Books by Tahir Shah:

A Son of a Son
Beyond the Devil's Teeth
Casablanca Blues
Casablanca Blues: The Screenplay
Congress With a Crocodile
Cultural Research
Eye Spy
Godman
Hannibal Fogg and the Supreme Secret of Man
House of the Tiger King
In Arabian Nights
In Search of King Solomon's Mines
Jinn Hunter: Book One – The Prism
Jinn Hunter: Book Two – The Jinnslayer
Jinn Hunter: Book Three – The Perplexity
Journey Through Namibia
Paris Syndrome
Scorpion Soup
Sorcerer's Apprentice
The Afghan Notebook
The Anthologies
The Caliph's House
The Clockmaker's Box
The Middle East Bedside Book
The Reason to Write
Three Essays
Timbuctoo
Timbuctoo: The Screenplay
Trail of Feathers
Travels With Myself
Travels With Nasrudin

THE ARABIAN NIGHTS ADVENTURES

A Story

TAHIR SHAH

THE ARABIAN
NIGHTS
ADVENTURES

A Story

TAHIR SHAH

MMXXI

Secretum Mundi Publishing Ltd
Kemp House
City Road
London
EC1V 2NX
United Kingdom

www.secretum-mundi.com
info@secretum-mundi.com

First published by Secretum Mundi Publishing Ltd, 2021
VERSION 06112020

THE ARABIAN NIGHTS ADVENTURES

© TAHIR SHAH

Visit the author's website at:

Tahirshah.com

ISBN 978-1-912383-62-7

For Sebastian
A magical boy, and a bridge –
Between Occident & Orient

One

SEIZED BY THE royal guard, the queen was dragged from the palace, and out to a bare patch of ground beyond the city walls…

…A patch of ground damp with blood.

The hood was jerked down into place.

A warrant bearing the king's coat of arms was presented to the executioner.

The prisoner was ordered to kneel.

Her delicate neck was forced against the wooden block, her nightdress flapping in the breeze.

Wheeling up into the dawn light, the axe fell.

Without ceremony or remorse, the queen's limp body was interred beside a thousand others.

As it was lowered into the grave, a desert wind tinged with dread tore through the capital.

Every young woman yet to be married was hidden away, for fear she'd be sent an invitation to her own wedding – a marriage to the cold-blooded King Shahriyar.

A marriage that invariably ended the same way – in a dawn appointment with the executioner's axe.

Yet another queen for a single night.

Two

A PALL OF terror hung over the land.

The king's spies were everywhere – searching for young women to be married at sunset, then executed at dawn. No one dared go out of their homes, in case an informant remembered they had a daughter, a sister, cousin, or niece.

Some families disguised their girls as boys, and smuggled them over the mountains to far-off lands. Most simply locked them away, refusing to allow them out, in fear theirs would be the next delicate neck on the executioner's block.

In the shadow of the palace, the king's vizier, Jafar, was sitting at the window of his home, pondering yet again how to put the bloodbath to an end. His wife blustered in, broke down in tears, and implored her husband to plead with the king.

'There's nothing I can do,' he answered. 'He's made up his mind. However hard I try, I can't talk sense into him. As you know, he's vowed to continue in this way – vengeance for the queen's infidelity.'

At that moment, the vizier's daughter entered. Her name was Scheherazade, and she was the apple of his eye. As keenly quick-witted as she was beautiful, she was blessed with a radiance that touched all who met her.

In her hand was a magnificent unopened envelope, her name inscribed beautifully on the front.

As soon as he saw it, the vizier choked back tears.

Unlike her father, Scheherazade didn't seem fearful so much as resolute.

'Dearest father,' she said, her tone reflective, 'I've made my decision.'

Her father stared deep into his daughter's eyes.

'I shall have a doctor swear that you're deranged!' he cried. 'Or have you smuggled over the border!'

'No, father,' Scheherazade answered. Opening the envelope, she read her name on the wedding invitation. 'I shall agree to his wishes, and be the king's next bride.'

Jafar leapt up.

'No no no!' he wailed, pulling his beloved daughter close, and scolding her at the same time. 'Put such senseless thoughts out of your head at once!'

But Scheherazade was adamant.

'If I don't wed him, another girl will be beheaded at dawn,' she said.

Bereft, the vizier replied:

'But at least it wouldn't be *my* daughter's head that falls.'

All morning, Scheherazade pleaded with her parents, and all morning they refused to let her be wed to the tyrannical king.

After what seemed like an eternity of argument, she motioned to the window. A splendid blue butterfly was flapping inside the glass, desperately trying to escape.

'See how it yearns to reach its destiny,' she said, opening the window.

Her father frowned as the insect flapped out into the sky.

'A pigeon could feast on it as soon as it's free.'

Scheherazade smiled.

'But, what if, by some strange quirk of fate, that little butterfly could prevent all the other butterflies from being trapped?'

And so it was that, with much sorrow, the vizier and his wife agreed to allow their daughter to wed King Shahriyar.

Three

As WORD OF the engagement was proclaimed throughout the kingdom, and a trousseau was prepared, Scheherazade took one last stroll alone through the market.

Covering herself with a simple cloak, she slipped out from the back door, promising to be back in time for the procession to the palace at dusk.

But rather than heading into the city, Scheherazade made her way in the opposite direction. Her feet moving as briskly as they could manage, she ventured over the river, across the floodplain, and into the forest.

Every parent warned their children to keep far away from that place, for fear that the witches living there would turn them into frogs. The ears of every child in the kingdom had heard stories of the dark arts, and had nightmares of the sorcery lurking there.

Every single child was terrified, that is, except the vizier's daughter.

While the other children followed their parents' advice, Scheherazade had always been the sort of girl who walked a path of her own.

And that was how she'd first met the kindly Blue Witch.

Over the years, since first straying into the forest and getting lost, Scheherazade had been taken in by the sorceress, and they had become firm friends. They told each other stories, laughed together, and confided in one another.

As always, the Blue Witch felt Scheherazade approaching,

sensed her small feet pacing fast through the forest. Once she had greeted the girl and ushered her into the shack in which she lived, she said:

'You are as brave as you are beautiful, my dear, and equally foolish.'

A single tear welled up in Scheherazade's eye and rolled down her cheek.

'I must stop him,' she whispered. 'I must put an end to King Shahriyar's killing spree.'

The Blue Witch thought long and hard, her gaze tethered to the floor.

'If only he could be halted by magical means,' she said at length. 'But, alas, the king is protected by Yunan, a sorcerer whose wizardry overshadows my own. Unlike the black arts he wields, I cast white magic – spells spun for good.'

Scheherazade was about to say something, when the Blue Witch clapped her hands together.

The kingdom, and everything in it, paused by a spell of white magic, in which only good deeds could be done.

In the market, all the sellers and the buyers, the chickens and the goats, were unmoving. Up in the trees, the birds were still, too. And, in his palace, King Shahriyar was motionless, a forefinger raised above his head.

Even Scheherazade was frozen to the spot.

Taking advantage of the spell she'd cast, the Blue Witch set to work.

First, she hurried out into the forest and gathered ingredients.

Next, she prepared a fine powder – grinding up barks,

crushing petals, and calling upon the Six Jinns to breathe life into her spell.

An hour after her hands had clapped, they did so once again, and the kingdom continued as though time and life were just as they had always been.

Filling a little embroidered pouch with the powder, the Blue Witch pressed it into Scheherazade's hand.

'Take this with you, and hide it with your trousseau,' she said. 'Follow the instructions I shall give you, and on no account reveal them to a living soul.'

Four

As the sun slipped down below the city wall, Scheherazade was conveyed to the palace upon a litter.

Trumpets resounding, the shrill voices of the wedding party called out in joy. Beneath the semblance of merriment were sorrow, fear, and heavy hearts. The vizier, his wife, and second daughter accompanied the procession as it swept through the courtyards into the throne room.

There, dressed in regal finery, the king was waiting for his bride.

Within minutes, the ceremony was over, and Scheherazade was queen.

Trumpeters heralded the union.

The wedding party congratulated their daughter, and said their farewells.

In tears, the vizier hugged his daughter, breathing in her perfume one last time.

As they prepared to leave, Scheherazade asked a favour of her husband.

'Would you permit my little sister, Dunyazad, to unpack my trousseau?'

The king agreed, and the ground beneath the newlyweds' feet was sprinkled with rose petals as they made their way to the private quarters.

There was no one in the kingdom who hadn't heard talk of the monarch's extravagance and wealth. But it was not until Scheherazade set eyes on the royal apartment that

11

she grasped the full extent of her husband's indulgence.

The walls were hung with the finest silks from distant lands, and the furniture was inset with precious gems. Exquisite mosaic fountains trickled with coloured water, solid-gold vases stood as tall as a man, and magnificent carpets from Samarkand were laid one over the next. Crystal chandeliers threw shadows over the scene plucked from a fairy tale, the air scented with the fragrance of musk.

While Dunyazad set to work unpacking her sister's possessions, King Shahriyar paced over to a low table upon which an ornate hourglass was standing. He gazed at his new bride for a moment, his eyes burning like fire opals.

Then, grasping the hourglass in both hands, he turned it over.

A fine stream of sand from the deserts of Arabia began to fall.

'Dearest husband,' said Scheherazade, 'I'm cold. Might a brazier be brought so that I could warm myself?'

The king clapped his hands and roared an order. A fire was brought in, coals clicking and sparking as they warmed the air.

'Any other requests?' asked Shahriyar. Cocking his head to the hourglass, he added: 'Time is against us as you know.'

Having finished unpacking the trousseau, Dunyazad stepped over to where her sister was sitting, and whispered something in her ear.

The king narrowed his eyes.

'What does she want?'

'Oh, nothing, husband.'

'It was something, so it wasn't nothing.'

'Well, nothing of importance.'

'Speak it and I shall decide.'

Scheherazade blushed from embarrassment.

'Forgive her,' she replied. 'My sister merely asked whether I would tell her a story before she leaves. You see, it's a tradition in our home. I tell her a tale each night before she sleeps. As she can't be certain when she shall see me again, she hoped that I might oblige.'

King Shahriyar smiled, the first time his new bride had observed him do so. Seating himself on a jewel-encrusted divan, he motioned for her to continue.

Thanking her husband, Scheherazade stepped over to the brazier, warming her hands on the embers. In doing so, she cast a pinch of the powder given to her by the Blue Witch onto the coals.

For a moment, the room was perfumed with an aroma unlike any other – a scent of raw imagination and destiny.

Glancing over to the hourglass, the sands of time flowing fast, she began:

'There was once in far-off China a tailor's son named Aladdin, who lived with his mother in the dark years after his father's death. Theirs was an impoverished life without luxury, balanced on the margins of starvation.

'One day, a wealthy stranger arrived at their modest home. Greeting Aladdin, he declared he was the boy's long-lost uncle. As a member of the family, he showered the boy and his mother in affection, presenting them with finery from his travels…'

Pausing, Scheherazade peered into the brazier's embers.

'Is that it?!' bellowed the king.

'No, no, there's more. There is *much* more. But…'

'*But?*'

Uneasily, the young bride cast an eye over to the hourglass, a mound of sand having gathered in the lower sphere.

'But I don't imagine you would wish to hear of it on your wedding night.'

The king clapped his hands.

'Continue!' he boomed.

Five

ALL NIGHT LONG, Scheherazade spun the tale, summoning the sounds, sights, and smells so vividly that it was as though the story were taking place right there in the royal apartment.

No surprise of course, for the Blue Witch's spell had been to conjure the tale in all its fantastical detail, as the sands in the hourglass fell.

King Shahriyar listened to his bride's voice. Or, rather, he thought he listened to her. In actual fact, he was watching the story unfold in a scene conjured by the brazier's fire.

As the first strains of dawn light brought warmth to the sleeping city down below, Scheherazade paused, her gaze gliding onto the hourglass.

The last grain of sand slipped through its neck, signalling the time for execution. Right on cue, the royal guard marched through the palace to drag the new queen to meet her fate.

Tears welling in her eyes, Dunyazad looked at her sister.

'I am ready,' Scheherazade said in a low voice.

The king frowned.

'But I haven't heard the end of the story,' he said.

The chief vizier stood to attention at the door of the royal apartment.

'Your Majesty,' he spoke sombrely, setting eyes on his beloved daughter, 'the executioner is ready, his axe sharpened, and the grave freshly dug.'

The frown on the monarch's brow grew more furrowed.

'But I want to know how it ends,' he said vacantly.

Scheherazade and her sister swallowed hard.

The vizier exhaled.

Raising a forefinger above his head, the king pronounced:

'Today there will be no execution,' he said. 'This evening I shall hear the last segment of the tale. Once it's finished, the axe may swing and the grave be filled.'

Six

ON THE SECOND evening, the hourglass was turned once again, grains of sand streaming through the slender neck of the magnificent device.

Dunyazad sat on the floor, the king on the low divan, and Scheherazade at the brazier, warming her hands. Although as quick-witted as she was lovely, the young queen's mastery in recounting the tale was inspired by the Blue Witch's enchantment.

Sprinkling a second pinch of the magic powder on the coals, Scheherazade continued the tale:

'And so it was that the boy born a tailor's son lived in luxury, with all the sweetmeats he could eat, and with a princess for his wife. All was well. Indeed, all was perfect. Then, one day, Aladdin quit the city on urgent business, leaving his wife to take care of their palatial home. With her husband gone, she was prone to boredom, and spent her days at the window, staring out at life on the street.

'On a particularly dull afternoon, she heard a tinker calling out as he pushed a cart. Unlike the usual assortment of worn-out pots and pans that tinkers tended to collect, this one was quite different. From what the princess could see, his cart was heaped with beautiful lamps made from the finest brass.

'"Old lamps for new!" he cried. "Come, quick, old lamps for new!"

'"That sounds like a wonderful bargain," the princess

17

said to her maid. "Take that wretched old lamp of my husband's and see whether the tinker would exchange it for one of those lovely new lamps on his cart."

'Hurrying down with Aladdin's lamp, the maid returned in less time than it takes to tell, a shiny new lamp in her hands.'

All night Scheherazade spun the tale, the sands of the hourglass streaming through its neck towards the dawn. And all night long her sister and the king watched as the tale was enacted right there before them.

With only a handful of grains still to fall, the queen drew the story of The Wondrous Lamp to a close:

'Although Aladdin and the princess lived happily ever after,' she uttered, 'the same cannot be said for the tailor.'

King Shahriyar shrugged.

'Which tailor?'

'Aladdin's uncle.'

'The wretch of a man who tricked him?'

'No, Sire, the real uncle... the one who left his tailor shop to his sons. The first son, Ali Baba, was kindly but poor; and the second was rich. While Qasim enjoyed a life of privilege, having managed to trick a woman of high birth to marry him, the first brother, Ali Baba, was resigned to work as a woodcutter.

'While at rest one blistering afternoon in the forest, he heard the sound of horses' hooves galloping towards him. Fearing it was the outriders of an army approaching, Ali Baba hid in a blasted tree. Peering through a slit in its side, he watched as forty thieves dismounted from their steeds, and strode up to a rock wall. "Open Sesame!" they cried. As the humble woodcutter watched, a great stone portal lifted upwards, revealing a secret cave, into which the thieves strode.

'A little time passed. The thieves exited, mounted their horses, and rode away as fast as they had come. When they were long gone, Ali Baba emerged from his hiding place, tramped timidly to the rock wall, and said the magic words. Instantly, the portal slid upwards, and Ali Baba entered the cave, filled as it was with the vast treasure of an empire.'

Scheherazade paused, as the last grain of sand slipped through the neck of the hourglass.

The sound of the royal guard approaching was followed once again by the voice of the chief vizier.

'Your Majesty, the executioner is waiting, and the grave freshly dug.'

Swallowing hard, the young queen glanced at her husband.

'There shall be no execution today!' he bellowed. 'It shall be postponed until tomorrow, once I have heard what happens to Ali Baba and the forty thieves.'

His eyes glazed over, the vizier bowed.

'At your service, Majesty,' he said.

Seven

NEXT EVENING, SCHEHERAZADE continued with the tale, grains of sand spilling through the hourglass once again.

As on the previous two nights, she sprinkled a pinch of the magic powder on the brazier's embers, conjuring the story to life within the fire. And, as on the other nights, the king had no comprehension that what he was witnessing was reality. In his mesmerized state, he assumed he was simply listening to his bride's silken words.

All night long, the tale was enacted, with Ali Baba surviving the murderous intentions of the forty thieves. The darkness waning beyond the palace window, a new tale began where the last came to an end. Utterly seamless and alluring, the story within a story gripped the king's attention like nothing he'd ever heard.

When the vizier appeared at the door the next morning, Shahriyar shooed him away.

'How would you ever expect my bride to be executed while the story of Sindbad the Sailor has yet to be told?'

Giving thanks to divine Providence, Scheherazade's father caught his daughter's eye in his. The hint of a smile on his lips, he confirmed the instructions.

Then, bowing, he excused himself.

Eight

AT THE FAR end of the kingdom, in a cave perched at the top of a desolate granite cliff, the sorcerer Yunan was reading the runes.

For a thousand years, his ancestral line had served that of King Shahriyar, protecting the royal house and vanquishing its foes. Peering into the embers of his fire, the great wizard grasped what Scheherazade was doing.

Clenching his right hand into a fist, he blew upon it, invoking the King of the Jinns. Once the supernatural creature had been summoned, his terrible form bearing down, the sorcerer spoke an order.

A flash of light, and the jinn was gone.

That evening, once he had attended to matters of state, the king took his place on the low divan and signalled for his bride to continue the story so newly begun, The Tale of Sindbad the Sailor.

Sprinkling a pinch of the magic powder on the brazier, Scheherazade spoke, and the story carried on where it had left off.

'Never has there been a sailor like Sindbad,' the queen announced. 'Unequalled in his bravery, his handsomeness, or in his kindness. In a marvellous dhow launched from the Arabian shore, he set out to the farthermost reaches of the East, guided by a million glinting pinpricks of light in the night sky.

'Shipwrecked on a desert island, his crew all drowned, the

great Sindbad scaled a cliff face and peered out. Nothing, from horizon to distant horizon. Nothing, but rolling waves and sea. Any other man might have been disconsolate, but Sindbad was in his element. Searching the cliffs, he came upon a giant nest – that of a roc, a bird the size of an elephant, summoned from the farthest limits of oblivion. To his amazement he saw that the nest contained a single, colossal egg. As he circumnavigated the nest, he heard the crazed screeches of the mother bird, flapping down from the heavens above.'

At that moment, the shutters were blown open.

A freezing breeze swept through the king's private chamber, the coals glowing bright red as it fanned them.

Scheherazade paused from her tale.

Sitting in her usual place on the floor, her sister rushed over and closed the shutters, as the king reached restlessly for a bunch of grapes.

Her concentration broken, the young bride repeated the previous line, and the story began playing out once again.

But, to her horror, the words she spoke were not the story that came alive.

With sand streaming through the neck of the hourglass in double-time, Sindbad the Sailor grasped the sword from his belt, and swung at the roc.

"'Die, you wretched creature!" he cried. "Wretched as King Shahriyar, the murderer of a thousand queens!'"

Realizing the words that had slipped across her lips, Scheherazade choked, her face blushing redder than red.

Across from her, the king was enraged, his complexion mirroring that of his bride.

'What?!' he bawled. 'Treachery!'

Thinking fast, the vizier's daughter made excuses, explaining she'd meant King Shahrigar, a monarch from the Mongolian Steppes.

The tension defused, the king tossed a grape into his mouth, and Sindbad's tale continued:

'Time and again, the roc attacked the sailor, her talons slashing like scimitars, her open beak screaking like a harbinger of death. As Sindbad battled to keep the bird at bay, Aladdin and Ali Baba appeared from nowhere. Imagine it! The three of them desperate to save their lives – like poor Scheherazade in the clutches of the wicked and ruthless tyrant, King Shahriyar!'

Nine

OVERCOME WITH WRATH, the monarch leapt up.

Hands clapping like cymbals, he bellowed at the top of his lungs for the royal guard. Crossing the room, he raised his fist to strike his bride. But, as he swung in her direction, the grains of sand in the hourglass froze.

Down in the city below, nothing moved, the world paused freeze-frame.

In the teahouses, customers sat mid-conversation, rigid like statues. In their homes, families were motionless. Above the streets, birds hung in the night air, as though time had come to an end.

In the king's apartment, the shadow of the Blue Witch roamed across the wall. Approaching Scheherazade, who was frozen as all the rest, she admonished the monarch for forcing such sorrow on his people. Then, whispering a spell, she cast a fistful of powdered antimony at the fire.

An explosion of light tore through the royal apartment.

Time and space were shunted on their axes, the silken walls melting into parched wilderness.

A sun hung like a great golden orb above an infinite desert. At the centre of the wasteland lay a secret caravanserai – a jumbled mess of tents plagued by flies, heat, and death.

On the northerly horizon, a dot was moving fitfully, like a flea vaulting about on a donkey's back. Gradually, it could be seen as what it was – a traveller riding a horse full tilt, as though his life depended on a message getting through.

Every few strides, his steed would buck and rear and, all too often, he would be thrown off, having to lure the poor creature back to him, and clamber on once again.

Due south of the encampment, a short, stout man was running through the sands, clothing shredded, his face a mask of desperation.

As the sun slipped to the edge of the earth, the two travellers reached the caravanserai and made their way to the one and only teahouse, with coarse carpets laid around it.

At the exact instant the two travellers arrived, the sound of a colossal bird high above drowned out the clamour of despondent camels.

Peering up into the last strains of dusk, the travellers watched as a young man tumbled from the clutches of a roc. He bounced onto the canopy of a goat-hair tent, and was thrown onto the carpets laid outside the teahouse – landing between the other two travellers.

'That was close,' the young man said, checking himself for injuries.

'What magic caused you to be up there in the heavens?' the stout traveller said in awe.

'Hitching a ride, that's all.'

'From where?'

'From way over there, across the desert. Only a madman would attempt it on foot.'

'I came by horse,' the other traveller stated arrogantly.

'I saw… You kept falling off!'

Recoiling in annoyance, the haughty traveller scowled.

'That's because I'm a sailor, and the desert I navigate is the ocean.'

The stout traveller pulled a scroll from his robe.

'I was ordered to come to this far-flung fragment of torment at this exact day and time.'

The sailor flinched.

'So was I,' he said, pulling a scroll from his saddlebag.

'And I,' said the young man who'd tumbled from the sky.

With no explanation why, the three travellers realized they'd each been ordered to arrive by dusk on the appointed day.

The traveller who'd come on foot explained that curiosity had brought him there.

The sailor echoed the reasoning.

The young man shrugged.

'Well, I'm afraid to tell why I came,' he said. 'Whoever wrote the message said they would turn me in to the royal guard for a certain misdemeanour.'

Just then, a woman's voice spoke from the gathering darkness:

'Each one of you has been summoned here for the same reason,' it said. 'Although your reasons for agreeing to come differ.'

'Curiosity,' said the first.

'Exactly, the same,' intoned the second.

'Nonsense,' said the voice. 'Sindbad the Sailor, you came because I threatened to reveal your darkest secret to the Emperor of Cathay. And, Ali Baba, you are here because I threatened to expose your secret to a certain sovereign – the one who's blind in the left eye. As for you, Aladdin, the list of your misdemeanours is so long there isn't a judge for a thousand horizons who wouldn't lock you up as soon as look at you!'

The three travellers squinted into the approaching night, trying to see where the voice was coming from.

'It's a phantom,' said Sindbad.

'It's a jinn,' whispered Ali Baba.

'It's a woman!' hissed Aladdin.

'Two of you are wrong,' said the voice, 'and one is right.'

The sound of someone clearing their throat caused the three travellers to turn around. Silhouetted against the campfire was the outline of a woman.

'Hello Sindbad, Ali Baba, and Aladdin,' she said. 'Consider yourselves introduced.'

'Who are you?' the sailor shot back.

'I am Scheherazade,' she said.

Ten

AS THE TRAVELLERS quenched their thirst and feasted on a meal of roasted goat, the queen explained why they'd been summoned.

'Despite your varied lives and adventures, the three of you are heroes in a collection of tales... the greatest treasury of stories ever set down by humankind.'

Aladdin peered at Scheherazade through the campfire's flames.

'What's its name?' he asked.

'It's called *The Thousand and One Nights*,' the queen replied. 'Or, rather, it will become known as that. You see, the story has not yet been told – so its very existence hangs in the balance, as does mine.'

'How so?'

'Because, unless the telling continues,' Scheherazade explained, 'my life, and those of countless other queens, will be snuffed out as sure as night follows day.'

Aladdin pushed a hand back through his hair.

'Don't know about the others, but I'm not a character from a storyland,' he said. 'I'm a man who has a past and a future.'

The queen rolled her eyes.

'That's what you think,' she said. 'Of course you had no idea of who or what you really are, just as you had no notion of each other's existence – or that my voice, guided by certain forces, has conjured you, and shaped each one of your tales.'

31

Tossing down a mutton bone, Ali Baba spoke for the others:

'If you're not a jinn, then what are you?'

'I am a queen – a queen married to a ruthless king. If the tale I tell falters, as it has apparently done, he'll execute me, and a thousand more women.'

Sindbad reached for another morsel of meat.

'And why should it have faltered?' he said. 'After all, a story's a story.'

Scheherazade peered out into the darkness, her mind reliving the predicament in which she found herself.

'The story's been diverted by a sorcerer in the employ of the king. He's thrown it out of kilter. As a result, the only certainty is my appointment with the executioner and his axe at dawn. Once I'm gone, King Shahriyar will marry a fresh bride each sunset and bury her each dawn.'

Aladdin frowned.

'In what way has the story been disturbed?'

Scheherazade sighed.

'In our love for tales, we overlook how they work,' she said.

'They work because a storyteller speaks, and someone listens. It's as simple as that.'

'No,' the queen replied. 'If that were true, then we wouldn't be in the quandary we're in. You see, when a tale is begun, a seed is planted, a seed from which the story grows and grows. Sometimes the seed ripens into a little story – a handful of words. But, at other times, it matures into a fantastical reflection of wonder.'

'What's the seed got to do with any of us?' Ali Baba asked.

'All three of you are heroes in a vast and intricate tale, a story that's a labyrinth of astonishment – the most complex tale ever told. Although I have only just begun recounting it, the twists, turns, and each individual adventure is contained within the story seed. Hide the seed, and the tale goes awry.'

'How would anyone hide a story's seed?' Sindbad snapped. 'It sounds preposterous, as though it were out of a story itself!'

'Of course it sounds as though it's from a story,' Scheherazade cried, 'because it *is*! As for how the seed of a story can be hidden, it's done through supernatural means. In this case, by the King of the Jinns.'

The sailor winced.

'I wish you luck,' he said. 'But I have a voyage to attend to.'

'And I have a shop to run,' Ali Baba mumbled.

'If you don't help me,' said the queen, 'I could have you both thrown into the deepest, darkest dungeon in any of a dozen kingdoms.'

Silence prevailed, eventually broken by Aladdin:

'Nothing would please me more than to be part of your quest,' he said with a smile.

Begrudgingly, the other two agreed, too.

'Excellent,' Scheherazade said. 'We leave at dawn.'

'Where to?' the sailor asked.

'To the City of Brass!'

Eleven

LONG BEFORE THE first blush of desert light warmed the travellers' faces, Scheherazade woke the others one by one.

During the few hours of rest, dreams transported them far from the freezing, flea-infested caravanserai.

Sindbad dreamt he was in a palace in distant China.

Aladdin imagined he was in a fantastical treasure cave.

Ali Baba fantasized he would one day own the most colossal marketplace for goods from all corners of the world.

Before they set out, Scheherazade explained that the City of Brass was the destination because the kindly Blue Witch had revealed it was from there the story's seed had been taken. On hearing the information, Sindbad clenched his hands into fists.

'You speak of witches, and claim to have power over us,' he said, straightening his back imperiously, 'but how do we know your power until we've seen it?!'

Scheherazade rolled her eyes.

'I am the teller of the story, of *your* story,' she replied. 'So I can control each one of you as I wish.'

With that, she pointed to the sailor.

'And the queen pointed to Sindbad the Sailor,' she said, 'her right hand clenched as a fist. Twisting it, she caused him to rise from the ground and turn in mid-air, hanging there like a bird in flight.'

As she spoke, Sindbad rose from the ground, and turned upside down.

'Put me down!' he cried.

'With pleasure,' said Scheherazade.

She clicked her fingers, and the sailor fell head first onto the sand.

Ali Baba stepped forward.

'Your Magnificence,' he said, fawning, 'I would be most obliged if you wouldn't use such necromancy ever in our presence.'

Aladdin and Sindbad seconded the request.

'Are you certain that's your wish?' Scheherazade said.

The three travellers nodded in unison.

'Please swear it in an oath,' they said all at once.

'Very well. I, Scheherazade, reluctant wife of King Shahriyar, pledge on all I hold sacred that while in your presence I shan't use the powers at my disposal as a storyteller.'

With that, the procession pushed out of the caravanserai.

Twelve

As THE FIRST rays of dawn light broke across the horizon, three dozen camels moved over the vast emptiness, a giant shadow thrown by each one.

Scheherazade led the way, the travellers behind her, and a retinue of pack animals and their attendants following at the rear. The frail light of dawn was quickly replaced by the piercing blaze of late morning, and heat so intense that it scorched any skin left unprotected.

Their heads furled in turbans, the ends tied over their faces, the humans were hopelessly unprepared for life in the parched wasteland.

Time and again Sindbad missed his footing and fell from his mount, to the amusement of the others.

'I'm a man of the sea!' he bawled. 'Put me on the ocean and you will know my skill.'

The sailor may have been unsure in his footing, but his aptitude for navigation was second to none. Charting the way by the night sky, he pointed out the constellations to the others, regaling them at the nightly campfire with tales of his voyages.

'I have crossed seas with waves as great as mountains,' he said, 'and with whales that would swallow an entire ship if they had the will. I've sailed to the ends of the earth, swum with mermaids, and listened to the cries of the great *bahamut*, the immense sea creature which holds up the earth.'

'And what did you learn in all your adventures?' asked Scheherazade.

The sailor didn't reply at first. He stared into the embers, his mind zigzagging through all the narrow escapes.

'I learned to treat every day as the greatest wonder imaginable,' he answered.

Aladdin wiped a hand down over his youthful face.

'And what have *you* learned in your adventures?' he asked the queen.

She smiled.

'To understand the power of stories,' she said.

Thirteen

FOR SEVEN DAYS the caravan crossed the desert, scorched by day and frozen to the bone at night.

Each one wished they could be transported to their destination by magical means, or that they would wake to find they'd been dreaming all along.

As one day slipped into the next, the travellers' skin grew increasingly blistered, their bodies ravaged by lice. Not wishing to be considered soft by the others, each one of them put on a brave face, and pretended the going was good.

On the seventh evening, Sindbad stared up at the firmament, his eyes fixed on its tapestry of constellations. While the desert was immense, the night sky hanging above it was incomparable. Billions and billions of pinpricks, as though the sun was being shone through a baker's sieve.

At length, the sailor surveyed the darkness beyond the makeshift camp.

'A sandstorm's approaching from the east,' he said. 'Wind as strong as any I have encountered on the ocean.'

Ali Baba asked the question in everyone's mind:

'How do you know?' he said.

Throwing his head back, Sindbad the Sailor gazed at the heavens.

'The wind powers my sails,' he said. 'It sings to me, and scorns me. But, most importantly, it never lies.'

'When will it reach us?' Scheherazade asked.

Slowly, the sailor filled his lungs, then exhaled.
'At first light,' he said. 'It will come at first light.'

Fourteen

ALL NIGHT LONG, the travellers prepared for the wind.

Supplies were unpacked and repacked, secured beneath great sheets of canvas, and dug down into the sand. The camels had their hobbles untied, and their heads wrapped in long strands of cloth.

Scheherazade climbed up onto a high dune overlooking their makeshift encampment, sparks from the fire below spitting up into the night. The moon was full, casting an eerie aspect over the rippled surface of the sands. She thanked Providence for saving her neck, if only for a few hours longer than was planned.

She thought of her mother and father, her beloved sister, Dunyazad, and of the ruthless man she'd married out of selflessness rather than love.

Perched up on the dune, she removed her turban so as to tie her hair back. As she did so, a stray strand of hair blew over her face. A moment later, she felt coolness on the back of her hand. Then, far in the distance she heard the faintest rumble of noise. A hissing sound, like a child blowing hard through a clenched fist.

The sailor called everyone to gather around.

'It's coming,' he said sombrely. 'Dig yourselves down as I showed you, and don't dare emerge until the uproar has come and gone.'

Aladdin asked how long it would last.

'No way of knowing,' Sindbad answered. 'All I can say

41

is that once it's passed by, we shall all be ripened by the experience.'

So each one of the travellers dug themselves in, as the first gusts reached the encampment, fanning the fire as though they were flames from the inner reaches of hell.

An hour of utter tranquillity came and went.

Then the full force of the sandstorm tore through in an ultimate performance of nature's rage.

All night it howled and bayed, screaming like a pack of wolves ten thousand strong. From time to time it would ease, then revive six times as forcefully as before.

At the height of the impact, a pair of the camels careered away and were soon engulfed. Breaking orders to dig in, one of the attendants went after them. Every inch of clothing, then skin, was stripped from his body, like a shaft of wood whittled beside a winter fire.

Through the next night the sandstorm raged on, and all through the following day. Her ears ringing, and her bones shaken until they were numb, Scheherazade prayed for tranquillity. But, the more she did so, the more the winds whipped up, howling with incandescent rage.

Three days and nights after the strand of hair had first blown across Scheherazade's face, the wind ceased. Not a gradual cessation, but rather an immediate end, leaving those who had experienced it wondering whether it had ever taken place at all.

Sindbad the Sailor was the first to emerge.

His muffled voice was heard by the others, calling them to come out.

'It's over! It's over!' he cried triumphantly.

One by one, the other travellers unfurled themselves, the blinding light dazzling them. Bewildered like victims from some forgotten war, they were reunited.

'I hate the desert,' Sindbad said. 'Take me to the sea!'

The remaining camels were calmed and attended to, and the supplies dug out from the pools of sand. Then, the sun blazing from an indigo sky, came the shrill sound of a voice in exclamation.

'Come! See! Quickly, all of you!'

Fearing another onslaught of nature's wrath, the other travellers followed the voice and were soon scrambling up a steep dune. Aladdin was standing at its apex, a hand shading his face.

'What is it?' Ali Baba yelled. 'Do you see the City of Brass?'

The boy pointed to the distance.

One by one, the others climbed up and set eyes on what he had discovered.

'Never in all my voyages!' yelled Sindbad.

'By what supernatural incantation...?' added Ali Baba.

Scheherazade said nothing.

Flabbergasted, she stood there, gazing out at the plateau stretching from the hillock to the horizon.

Through days and nights the wind had stripped the desert away, revealing a colossal city, entombed, like a wonder from the pages of a child's fantasy. Every single grain of sand had been sucked out – millions and billions of tons of powdered rock.

The result was a city deserted of all life, but preserved in entirety, as though everyone had crept away and never returned. Like dreamwalkers lured by curiosity, the four travellers hurried down into the metropolis.

Too awed to say a word, each one seemed to glide forward as though silenced by a spell. Descending into the maze of streets, they found shops filled with their wares, the workshops of scribes ready for clients, guard posts neat and orderly, and carpenters' yards ready and waiting.

'Where are all the people?' Aladdin asked.

'*Dead?*' suggested Scheherazade.

'How could they be?' Ali Baba answered.

'They're not dead, but gone,' Sindbad said.

Aladdin balked.

'Gone *where?*'

'Who knows?' murmured Sindbad.

'A jinn,' said Scheherazade. 'This is the work of a jinn. A city as great as any in all the world, transported to nowhere – for the senseless amusement of a jinn.'

Aladdin was pointing again.

'Look, the shops are filled with merchandise.'

A mask of the most terrible fear swept down over Scheherazade's face.

'Do not take a thing! Not a single thing! D'you hear me?!'

'Why not?' Ali Baba asked.

'Because this scene smacks of diabolical sorcery. We can't risk unleashing the rage of whoever, or whatever, cast such a despicable spell.'

Exploring the streets, they marvelled at the bolts of cloth in the tailors' shops, the coloured goblets neatly arranged in the glass-blower's studio, and the cabinets of gold jewellery on display in a bridal emporium.

'To think we would have simply marched across it, not knowing it was here,' Aladdin voiced in wonder.

'It must have lain here for centuries,' Sindbad replied.

Scheherazade gazed up at the sun.

'We must get the camels ready and keep going,' she said.

Making their way back through the streets, the travellers began ascending the steep dune back to where their camp was pitched.

As they climbed, there was a clap of thunder.

'The wind! The wind!' Ali Baba yelled. 'It's coming back again!'

His face cloaked in fear, the sailor pointed upwards.

'It's not the storm,' he said.

One at a time they looked upwards, their heads cocking back hard as they followed the mountainous trunk of a creature's form.

As wide as a building, it seemed to rise up into the heavens, swathed in a filthy, blood-splattered robe. In places the garment was so badly torn that the travellers caught a glimpse of the flesh beneath. Scaled and wart-ridden, it was like the hull of a ship that had been at sea for many months.

Far above the creature's trunk were four arms, each one grasping a blood-soaked scimitar, and finally a head so monstrous it defied description – except to say it was crowned by a pair of razor-sharp horns.

Before any one of the group had mustered a sentence, the creature spoke, his voice booming with fury:

'Who dares steal from the Black Jinn?'

Standing tall, Scheherazade replied:

'Oh great and mighty creature from the heavens, please rest assured that none of us would take a single grain of rice from the city that lies below. We merely explored it, and marvelled at the power that transported it to this distant realm.'

'Nooooooo!' cried the Black Jinn, all four arms raised above his head, scimitars flashing like demons. 'One of you has stolen, and all of you shall pay!'

Quickly, Scheherazade conferred with the others.

'I took nothing,' Sindbad affirmed.

'Nor I,' Ali Baba added.

Aladdin swallowed anxiously.

'The tiniest little button,' he whispered, opening his fist. 'The smallest memento. I'm sorry… it just caught my eye.'

'You wretched boy!' the sailor growled. 'For your stupidity we'll lose our heads!'

High above them, the Black Jinn rankled with rage, his anger boiling over to fever pitch.

Again, Aladdin spoke to the others:

'If our storyteller used the powers she possessed, then we might have a chance at living!'

'But what could she do?' Ali Baba moaned.

'She could tell the tale in another way!'

All eyes turned to Scheherazade.

Arms crossed, the queen shook her head left, right, left.

'On your orders I made an oath on all I hold sacred!'

'Then we shall die,' said Ali Baba. 'Slaughtered like the wretches we surely are.'

His prey the size of vermin on the desert's face, the Black Jinn heard their voices as humans hear mice.

'What's with all this bickering?!' he cried.

The travellers froze.

Then, finding humour in their predicament, Aladdin broke into fits of laughter.

'We're just blaming the storyteller among us for not changing the story.'

The jinn frowned, lowering his head until it was in line with the travellers' faces, a single grotesque eye straining to focus on them.

Each one of them grimaced at seeing the eye, and smelling such truly abominable breath.

'Storyteller?!' he called. 'Which one of your vile excuses for life is a storyteller?'

Without fear, Scheherazade raised her hand.

'I am.'

'Then you shall die first!'

The queen shrugged.

'Might I ask what you have against storytellers?'

The Black Jinn's scimitars slashed left and right, narrowly missing the travellers.

'I shall hack you into morsels, grind your bones into dust, then blow it to all four points of the compass!'

Scheherazade held her ground.

'You didn't answer my question,' she yelled. 'What do you have against the noble art of storytelling?'

His face no more than a few yards from the group, he said:

'For a thousand years I have been the butt of every joke spoken by storytellers' mouths. I have been ridiculed, maligned, and called a stinking, wretched excuse of life!'

'I'm sorry that's what others have called you,' Scheherazade said. 'But I myself have sung your praises, and named you as the handsomest, proudest, kindest jinn that ever walked the roaming sands of Arabia.'

'Nonsense!' cried the Black Jinn. 'You're as bad as all the rest of them, and you shall perish first!'

Irked that he was to die in the desert and not the sea, Sindbad the Sailor spoke:

'O Great Jinn, O towering pillar of life and extinguisher of evil! By freeing us, you will prove your good, and will be regarded as a saint evermore by spinners of yarns, and tellers of tales!'

An expression of meekness slipped over the creature's face.

'Is that true?' he asked.

Fifteen

IN THE BLINK of the Black Jinn's eye, the four travellers were pinned out on the desert sands with leather bindings, spreadeagled like skins at a tannery left out to dry.

'Damn you, Aladdin!' the sailor bellowed. 'There's no honour in dying here, like this!'

'He couldn't help it,' Ali Baba broke in. 'Any one of us might have allowed their hand to stray.'

'It was such a lovely little button,' Aladdin moaned.

Again, all three men begged Scheherazade to retell the tale, without the Black Jinn.

'I can't and I won't!' she shouted. 'So don't ask me again!'

Aladdin began cackling once more.

'We're not going to get a chance to!'

Curious that anyone but a madman would find humour in their fate, the jinn lowered his head inquisitively.

'Why does the young one laugh?' he asked.

'Because the storyteller over there could paint you in words as a picture of wonder and delight,' said Sindbad, 'but she refuses to do so.'

'And why is that?' the Black Jinn enquired.

Ali Baba explained:

'Because she had made an oath on all she holds sacred,' he said, 'and unlike the rest of us she won't break it, even though her neck's on the line.'

The jinn gazed at Scheherazade pinned out on the sand.

'I loathe storytellers more than any form of life...

49

even more than the Turquoise Jinn from the Kingdom of Astamagar.'

Doing her best to be diplomatic, the queen said:

'Beloved Black Jinn, who holds our lives in his hand, what if we could change the way others regard you?'

'Are you offering to describe me differently?' he asked, his brow furrowed deep.

'No,' Scheherazade answered. 'Your story has already been told.'

'Then what's there to be done?'

'Well,' said the queen softly, 'my friends and I would like to clean you up, and dress you in clothing fit for a jinn as distinguished and handsome as yourself.'

The Black Jinn growled.

'What good would that do?'

'It would make others wish to be near you for a start, and would give you back your sense of self-respect.'

'How can you be sure it'd work?'

'Well, if it doesn't, you could simply stake us out on the desert again.'

The creature brooded long and hard.

Then, he clicked his tongue. Instantly, the leather bindings vanished, and the prisoners were free.

Sixteen

WITH THE BLACK Jinn's permission, the travellers led half a dozen camels down into the deserted city, and loaded them up with merchandise.

Late in the day they returned, the beasts burdened under the weight of cloth, leather, soap, and perfume. All night they scrubbed the jinn, chipping away at centuries of filth. They trimmed his talons and cleaned his horns, shaved his face, brushed his teeth, and cut his hair.

All the while, the Black Jinn watched with annoyance, his single eye widening with disapproval.

'If I don't like it, I'll peg you out again and leave you to die!' he'd call from time to time, until Scheherazade barked back at him.

'Will you *shush*?!' she spat. 'In case you haven't noticed, we are doing this to help you, and to make others like you.'

'But what if I don't want anyone to like me?' the Black Jinn snapped.

'Well, then you'll turn into a sad, good-for-nothing old jinn! And you won't have lovely clothes to wear, like the ones my friends are making.'

The creature raised its head inquisitively.

'Show me the clothes,' he said.

'No! Not until they're finished. You'll like the surprise.'

Again, the Black Jinn growled.

'I hate surprises,' he whimpered testily, 'almost as much as I hate storytellers!'

Scheherazade, who had been sitting on the top of the creature's head, brushing back his hair, climbed down onto his shoulder. From this vantage point, she made her way onto his nose and peered into his eye.

'Why all the hatred for storytellers?'

'They're horrible!' the Black Jinn growled. 'He said horrifying things about me.'

'*They* or *he*?'

The jinn rolled his eye.

'*He!*'

'He *who*?'

'*He* the unkind storyteller in the market in Damascus.'

Scheherazade leant in close, her voice directed into the creature's ear.

'What did he say?' she asked tenderly.

'That I was ugly and stupid, and that I was the runt of my mother's litter.'

'Is it true? Were you the runt?'

The Black Jinn shook his head.

'No. I was the strongest from the day we were born.'

There was a whistling from the ground.

'Ah,' Scheherazade said, 'it's ready.'

'What is?'

'Come and see.'

Expert at making sails, Sindbad the Sailor had used his skill to craft a robe colossal in its proportions, sewing dozens of bolts of cloth side by side. Aladdin had trimmed the garment in gold beading, and had even embroidered *Black Jinn* on the front, surrounded by flowers. As for Ali Baba, he'd fashioned a pair of moccasins from forty goat skins.

Turning their backs to give the Black Jinn a little privacy, the travellers waited while he dressed himself. When he was ready, he materialized a pool of crystal-clear water in the desert, and peered into it.

'Don't you like it?' Scheherazade asked hesitantly.

The jinn snarled, growled, and snarled again, his face reflected over the surface of the water.

A single tear welled up in his eye, and rolled down the right side of his face.

'You've made an old jinn happy,' he said.

Sindbad the Sailor spoke up:

'You could have done all that yourself with magic.'

'Of course I could,' the Black Jinn retorted.

'Then why didn't you?'

'Because the pleasure is knowing that others cared,' he said.

'Does that mean we're free?' Aladdin asked.

'I suppose it does.'

The travellers let out a wail of joy, then Ali Baba asked the Black Jinn what his plans were for the future.

'Thought I'd go down to Africa and roast a few kingdoms,' he muttered dreamily.

Scheherazade shook a fist.

'If you want to be liked,' she scolded sharply, 'you have to be likeable. And roasting innocent people for no reason at all is no way to be likeable!'

Once again, Aladdin conferred with the others, and they all agreed.

TAHIR SHAH

'Why don't you come with us?' he asked.

'Where to?'

'The City of Brass.'

'That's a long way.'

'Not for you!'

The Black Jinn nodded.

'If I click my tongue, we'd get there right away.'

'No!' Scheherazade cried. 'No magic! You must promise it on all you hold sacred.'

'But why?'

'For the same reason I didn't escape your clutches by retelling the tale.'

'What's the reason?'

'Because there's more honour in it.'

Sindbad was staring out at the horizon. Turning he cried out:

'Think of it as a new beginning!'

The Black Jinn smiled – the first time he'd done so without causing harm to others.

'Very well,' he said. 'I shall come with you.'

Ali Baba raised an arm.

'As our travelling companion, is it too much to ask your name?'

Self-consciously, the Black Jinn touched a paw to his head, grooming back his hair.

'My mother named me Baibar,' he said modestly.

Scheherazade stepped forward and extended her hand.

'Pleased to meet you, Baibar,' she said.

Seventeen

FOR THIRTEEN HORIZONS the caravan continued, animals and men pacing through fiery mornings, and long, roasting afternoons in the Black Jinn's shadow.

Each night they would set up camp, and take it in turns to tell tales of their adventures.

One night, far cooler than the rest, Aladdin wrapped himself in an extra blanket and stoked up the fire.

'Who's going to tell a story tonight?' he asked.

Scheherazade motioned towards Baibar.

'Would you regale us with a tale?'

'I have nothing of interest to share,' the jinn replied meekly.

'Don't believe it for a minute,' the queen responded. 'I'm sure yours are the greatest stories of all.'

Baibar sighed.

'All right, but only if you promise not to make fun of me.'

'Just get on with it!' taunted Sindbad.

'Please,' Ali Baba said.

'We would be honoured,' Scheherazade added gently.

The Black Jinn began:

'I was born beyond the Slaked Kingdom,' he said, 'in a land so dry the mountains were bleached as white as whale bones. My childhood was a happy one. My siblings and I would fight with our swords through the nights, and spit poison at one another through the days. It was blissful.'

'Sounds like a delight,' Sindbad said caustically.

Scheherazade leaned over and thumped him.

'Please continue Baibars,' she whispered.

'Then one day the sky grew dark, as though a plague of locusts was approaching. We ceased our games, and watched. It soon became clear that it wasn't insects coming towards us, but a swarm of flying ogres.'

'Flying *ogres*?' whispered Aladdin.

'Yes. Thousands of them. They hurtled from the sky, attacking anything they could get their paws on. My father and mother were chopped into pieces, and my siblings and I were carried away.'

'Where to?' Ali Baba asked.

'To a kingdom beneath the ocean. It was there the flying ogres lived. They had a vast system of caves in which air had been trapped – a world of its own. My brothers, sisters, and I were forced to work down in the mines. The ogres had captured us, and thousands of other jinn children, because we were small and strong.

'They worked us day and night, month after month, year after year. One at a time my brothers and sisters gave in. You see, none of us had yet learned how to activate our powers. By the end, I was the only one left. Enraged, the ogres forced me to toil for my entire family. One night, unable to stand it any more, I made a bid to escape.'

'Did you get away?' Aladdin asked.

'Yes, I did. But the ogres came after me. No one had ever broken free before, and they went wild with ire. Swimming up from the ocean floor, I managed to reach the mainland. As you can imagine, everyone I encountered thought I would cause terror, and refused to help. And, as no one would give me food when I asked, I had no choice but to terrorize them for it.'

The Black Jinn rubbed a paw to his eye, blinked once, then again, and said:

'If you live as I do, it's remarkably easy to fall into an immoral pattern of life. I felt guilty at first,' he said, 'but then I suppose I got used to it. I may have become a good citizen, but then I met a Frost Jinn from the mountains, and there was no turning back. Not until now.'

'What's a Frost Jinn?' asked Ali Baba.

'The meanest, cruellest jinns that walk the earth. They make us Black Jinns look like pussy cats. He taught me how to activate my powers, and to work on them until I was on tip-top form.'

Sindbad cleared his throat.

'How does a jinn activate powers?'

'Squashing people is a good way to do it,' Baibar replied. 'Or flattening an entire city. That works wonderfully well.'

Scheherazade scowled.

'So, you mean through death, destruction, and causing misery to thousands of innocent people?'

The Black Jinn pondered for a moment.

'Yes, that's right,' he said. 'And with all the time I spent learning from the Frost Jinn, I got my powers in top-notch shape. I could run around the world in five minutes flat, scaring everyone in my path, or crush an entire kingdom in half that time. It was wonderful!'

'*Wonderful?*' the queen growled.

'Um, er, well, it was a way to live,' Baibar said. 'And it made me very strong. I never would have turned my back on that life, but something inauspicious happened.'

Aladdin shrugged.

'Something bad?'

'Yes.'

'What was it?' Scheherazade asked.

'The King of the Jinn,' Baibar said, his mouth drying from the words. 'It seemed that the Frost Jinn and I trespassed on his territory and he got so angry that the sun was too frightened to shine for an entire week. The world went completely black.'

'When was this?' asked Sindbad.

'More than eight hundred years ago. We went into hiding at the bottom of a very deep mine shaft. The poor old Frost Jinn made the mistake of sneezing so loudly that he got caught. But by sheer good luck I wasn't found. When I eventually came out, I was so weak that I had to squash dozens of kingdoms to get my strength back. A little later, a Blue Jinn bet I couldn't lift up a city, shake all the people off, then transport it into the middle of the desert.'

'Is that how the city came to be standing where it is?'

The Black Jinn nodded his great head.

'I liked the climate, so I stayed here for a while.'

'How long is a while?'

'Three hundred years,' Baibar said. 'I've been in the desert for three hundred years.'

'But there's no one for you to terrorize here,' Ali Baba pointed out.

'You'd be surprised,' the jinn responded. 'Keep your eye open and you come across plenty of lost travellers.'

Eighteen

THE SUN SEEMED to double its ferocity, and then double again.

Two full weeks after leaving the abandoned city, it became so hot that the travellers strained to breathe, each of them desperate for water. Hour after hour they trudged on. And hour after hour they imagined they'd seen glorious pools of ice-cold water beckoning them in the distance.

Unable to continue, Ali Baba climbed up the jinn's robe and hid in the pocket, until Scheherazade ordered him down.

'We can't risk reaching the City of Brass by magical means!' she snapped. 'If we do so, my head will be swiped off my shoulders, and a thousand more women will follow.'

'But taking a free ride isn't using magic,' Ali Baba answered tetchily.

'Maybe not to you, but we can't do anything that'll break the rules.'

'I've never heard it said that story seeds have rules attached to them,' Sindbad the Sailor broke in.

'I've never heard of story seeds,' Aladdin said.

The Black Jinn pointed to the distance.

'I can see water,' he said.

'Me too,' Ali Baba whimpered. 'The cool, delicious water of yet another mirage.'

'I've already jumped into it a hundred times,' the queen replied, 'at least I have in my imagination.'

One by one, the travellers tramped forwards, the mirage getting closer.

'This one's better than the others,' Sindbad chuckled. 'I can even hear the wind in the palms.'

'And I can smell the water,' Aladdin sighed.

'That's because it's a real oasis,' Baibar said.

Nineteen

WERE IT TO have existed in the middle of a bustling city, no one would have taken any notice of the oasis at all – but the fact it was surrounded by a sand sea, made it what it was...

An unrestrained paradise.

Having unloaded and watered the camels, the travellers jumped into the pool of pristine water, splashing and laughing like children in a bath. With mile-wide grins, they thanked Providence for answering their prayers, and for rewarding their misery with such joy.

Ali Baba scrabbled up the Black Jinn. Standing on his head, he plucked coconuts from the palms, and tossed them down.

'I'm never going to leave,' he yelled.

'Of course you are!' Sindbad cried back. 'This isn't a destination, but a teahouse in nature's finest caravanserai!'

Crossing the oasis, Scheherazade found a quiet corner in which to wash free from the gaze of others. She was busy cleaning herself when she spotted the outline of another woman doing the same in a copse of trees at the pool's edge. She was about to call out, when it dawned on her who the other person was.

Aladdin.

Dressing herself, the queen approached gingerly.

Hearing someone coming, Aladdin fumbled to get dressed.

'How could I not have known?' Scheherazade said with a smile. 'After all, it's me who's telling the story.'

Aladdin blushed.

'Please don't tell,' she said. 'Allow me to keep my secret.'

'But why do you hide the fact that you're a woman?'

'If it was known, then I'd be married to a tyrant, rather than out here on an adventure.'

The queen considered the words, her mind flashing with the portrait of her own husband.

'Your secret is safe with me,' she said.

The cries of a man's voice resounded from the far side of the palms.

Dressing themselves as quickly as they could, the others hurried over.

Still perched on the Black Jinn's head, Ali Baba had spotted something at the bottom of the pool…

The outline of a ship.

As though his prayers had been answered, Sindbad the Sailor dived into the water.

A handful of minutes passed, then he reappeared, gasping for air.

'It's a Chinese junk!' he exclaimed. 'I can't believe it!'

'How could a ship ever have got here, in the middle of the desert?' asked Ali Baba blankly.

'Same way that a city got buried under the sand.'

Baibar blinked meekly, dimples forming in either cheek.

'I could pluck it from the water,' he said.

Scheherazade forbade him, for fear it would disrupt the sequence of events that were to follow.

'See any treasure down there?' Aladdin asked.

Sindbad's eyes widened.

'Yes, I did.'

'Rubies, emeralds and gold?'

'I think you should all come down and see,' he said.

Twenty

ONE AT A time, the travellers swam down to the ship, lying on its side in a bed of fine silt.

And, one at a time, they discovered something even more unlikely than a ship at the bottom of a desert pool.

In the vessel's bow was an air pocket, in which an oracle resided behind a carved marble screen.

Sindbad took Ali Baba down first.

Although terrified, he begged the diviner to give a hint at the life he hoped to live.

'You shall receive blessings if you give blessings,' the voice spoke. 'Never rest until you have attended to others.'

Aladdin was the second to swim down.

'Your secrets will remain secrets if you strive to reach the ends of the earth. Give more than you take, and take less than you need.'

The sailor beckoned Scheherazade towards the pool.

'I'll show you how to reach the oracle,' he said.

'I have no need to know my future,' she answered.

'Why not?'

'Because doing so would surely dash my dreams to dust.'

Sindbad asked the Black Jinn whether he wished to know what was to come.

'In more usual circumstances I might agree,' he responded. 'But, given that it was I who caused the ship to be lying where it is, it may be rash of me to avail of its services.'

Ali Baba turned to the sailor.

'What awaits you?' he asked.

Sindbad's eyes seemed to cloud over.

'Strange things,' he said. 'Strange things.'

That night, when the camels, the jinn, and the other travellers were fast asleep, Scheherazade got up from her place beside the fire.

In the light of the moon, she stole down to the water's edge, waded in, and dived down.

Just as Sindbad had promised, she found the air pocket and the marble screen.

'O great oracle,' she said, 'I come in peace, a humble traveller on my way to the City of Brass.'

'I know your destination, just as I know your future and your past, Queen Scheherazade,' the voice spoke.

'Then you know that I am married to a tyrannical king who's already killed a thousand brides. And that mine is a journey made from desperation.'

'I know all truth,' the oracle replied.

'Then can you say whether I reach the city and retrieve the seed of the story that has been hidden there?'

The oracle did not answer.

Her voice tinged with desperation, Scheherazade repeated her question.

'Time is against you,' the voice hissed, after what seemed like an eternity of silence. 'You must leave and make haste.'

'We intend to quit the oasis at dawn,' the queen answered.

'That will be too late. You must leave at once!'

Her heart pounding with terror, she gave thanks, swum

out of the ship's side, and up through the silvery water.

'Wake up! Wake up!' she yelled, running to the others. 'We must leave! There's not a moment to delay!'

Hurriedly, the camels were roused and loaded, and the camp packed up.

'What's the panic?' Sindbad yelled.

Her hair still dripping, Scheherazade took in the sailor's silhouette.

'I feel it in my bones,' she said.

Twenty-one

BY FIRST LIGHT, the oasis was a distant memory.

Moving forward, the heat rising by the minute, the travellers moaned and groaned, and the pack camels did the same.

From time to time, Baibar would untie his turban and wring it out, unleashing a great pool of saltwater, which drained into the sand.

Always at the front, Scheherazade led the way over towering dunes and down through valleys between them, as though leading an army into war. Her pace didn't let up, not for an instant. Whenever the others cried out for her to slow, she would turn momentarily, and wave them forward.

Sindbad the Sailor only managed to keep going by pretending he was sailing a dhow across an open sea. But, as soon as he remembered where he was, he'd collapse onto the dunes and beg to be transported to anywhere but where he was.

Behind him, her strides becoming shorter and shorter, was Aladdin. A thousand times she'd imagined the others learning of her identity, and what they might have made of it. And a thousand times she thanked all she held sacred for freeing her from the savage binds of injustice.

As for Ali Baba, he had a secret of his own, one that kept his feet moving despite his body aching as though it had been torn to shreds and stuck together again. He may have been older and more corpulent than the others, but nothing could stop him.

Nothing, that is, other than what was to come.

Day and night they journeyed, halting no more than a few minutes each dawn, and the same again each dusk. The beasts of burden lurched from side to side with exhaustion, grunting and snorting as though the end of their lives had come.

Six days and six nights beyond the oasis, Baibar thrust all four arms into the air in jubilation.

'I see the city!' he boomed. 'I see the City of Brass!'

The words like sustenance from heaven, the travellers hastened forwards.

Three hours later each one of them caught their first sight of it – the outline of a city capped with magnificent gilded domes.

Soon after that, they were crossing the flood plain of a mighty river, glimpsing the first greenery they'd seen since the desert paradise.

Drawing closer, they spied flocks of fat-tailed sheep grazing in meadows of knee-high grass, and cows striding majestically towards the water's edge.

There were egrets, too, hundreds of them, their long bills rooting for worms in the soft soil. Most importantly though, there were people – milling about in the distance on donkeys, horses, or simply ambling through the lush landscape plucked from every desert traveller's imagination.

As they approached the last span of the flood plain, a

deafening noise drowned out the sounds of nature, and the sky darkened.

Something was hurtling down from the sky – what looked like a colossal, square-edged meteorite. Peering up into the heavens, the travellers watched as another massive stone shot down, fixing itself to the first.

Then another, and another.

'They're linking up!' Sindbad shouted.

They all watched in stupefaction, the ground shaking as one block joined up with the last.

'Baibar, strike them away!' Scheherazade yelled.

Following orders, the Black Jinn bounded forwards, all four arms swiping left and right, as though trying to swat a plague of flies.

Every time he tried to hit one of the blocks, it simply jerked out of the way, and came to a rest beside the others.

'A wall!' Aladdin bawled. 'It's building a wall!'

Scheherazade's face turned cherry-red with rage.

'The work of the sorcerer, Yunan!'

'We can climb it!' Aladdin said enthusiastically.

As the short sentence was spoken, the wall began growing from the ground. Within a single minute, it was so high that the sun had been blocked out.

Sindbad was the next to speak:

'Baibar, take off your shirt!'

The others looked round in puzzlement.

As requested, the Black Jinn removed his shirt.

Working double-speed, Sindbad tore the garment down the main seam, and curled the cloth around the tent poles.

Soon, he'd fashioned a kind of canopy, attaching four lengths of cord to it.

'This is where we leave the camels and attendants,' he explained.

Ali Baba screwed up his face.

'Are we going to magically lift into the air and float down the other side?' he asked.

'No magic!' Scheherazade barked.

'No, no,' the sailor confirmed. 'No magic! We'll tie ourselves on, and ask our dear friend Baibar to throw us over. There's no magic in that.'

'And let us plunge to our deaths?' Aladdin whined.

'No we won't. We'll float down.'

The queen stepped away from the others, cursing her husband, then his sorcerer. She was about to suggest they give the matter more thought, even though time was against them, when Baibar yelled out again.

'I think Sindbad's idea is a good one,' he said.

'And I think it could get us all killed,' Ali Baba replied.

'An imperfect plan today is better than a perfect plan tomorrow,' he replied.

'Are you a philosopher all of a sudden?'

The Black Jinn shook his head.

'No,' he answered. 'I'm just pointing out the obvious.'

With that, he jerked a paw behind him.

The travellers turned.

Ranging over the horizon in the desert's darkness was an army.

'They look like snake ghouls to me,' the jinn said.

'What the hell are snake ghouls?!' Sindbad cried.

'A pain in the backside,' Baibar groaned.

'Can't say I'd know, because I've never encountered them before.'

'That's obvious,' the Black Jinn shot back.

'Why?'

'Because if you'd ever met a snake ghoul before, you wouldn't be standing there looking at them coming towards you.'

Scheherazade stared at the approaching army, their fusillades of arrows getting closer and closer through the shadows. Then, turning one-eighty, she looked out at the great wall.

'Certain death,' she said, the word expressed without emotion.

Sindbad clapped his hands.

'Come on! Let's tie ourselves onto the sail and get thrown up over the wall! We'll be eating kebabs in no time!'

All eyes turned to the queen.

'All right,' she said, frostily. 'But only because we're out of choices.'

As quickly as he could, Sindbad knotted the others in place, and then himself.

'Sorry to be leaving you, Baibar,' he said.

'Don't worry about me,' the Black Jinn said with a grin, 'I'll get over there somehow and we'll have kebabs together.'

The snake ghouls were close now, their arrows and spears striking the ground all around the travellers.

'Hurry!' Sindbad cried. 'Cup us in your fist and throw us up with all your might!'

Baibar did as the sailor had asked him.

Scooping the others up in one of his four paws, he tilted back, and launched them full force into the air.

As though shot from a catapult, they climbed up into the sky.

But, rather than clearing the top of the wall, they slammed into it.

Shrieking in pain, they screamed as they fell.

The Black Jinn dived towards the wall, and managed to catch them just before they hit the ground.

Sindbad snarled:

'Try again, and put your back into it this time!'

The arrows were falling like rain now.

Grasping the travellers tight in his fist, his back covered in arrows, Baibar hurled the sail and its passengers up into the sky a second time.

Yet again, they slammed into the wall, and fell.

'Can't do it,' the Black Jinn groaned as he caught his companions. 'I don't have the strength.'

'How d'you get strength?' asked Ali Baba.

'By flattening kingdoms,' the jinn replied.

'Isn't there any other way?' asked Scheherazade, focussing on the army of snake ghouls, which was closing in.

'Causing terror and misery,' he said bashfully.

'Well, why don't you cause *them* a little terror and misery?!' Aladdin cried.

'Won't work.'

Aladdin balked.

'Why not?'

'Because they're magical beings, and magical beings don't count.'

Sindbad raised a forefinger.

'Do the jinn rules say what kind of kingdom it has to be?'

'No,' Baibar answered. 'Only that it must be "obliteration on a gigantic scale".'

The sailor's face seemed to brighten.

He pointed to a termite mound.

'Flatten that!' he yelled.

In one stride, Baibar had reached it, and crushed it.

'Ooooh,' he said contentedly, as a fusillade of spears hurtled down. 'Think that did it. I'm feeling revived.'

'*Strong* and revived?' Scheherazade asked.

'Very much so.'

'So throw us with all your might!'

Doing as the queen had bid him, the Black Jinn tossed the travellers up into the air – so high that they were covered in icicles. Peering down, they saw the wall far behind in the distance.

Then they fell. Or, rather they floated down in the canopy made from Baibar's shirt.

As they neared the city's outline, they called to one another, jubilantly.

'I can smell the kebabs roasting!' Aladdin wailed.

'And I can see the palace!' Ali Baba added.

'I'm going to take a bath!' Sindbad howled.

'And I'm going to find the story seed!' Scheherazade yelled.

Twenty-two

WHETHER IT WAS a case of the Black Jinn having aimed well, or plain good fortune, the canopy drifted down through the cloudless sky right above the city, its passengers blinded by dazzling light.

The streets so close below them, they could hear voices of the stall-keepers in the market touting vegetables, and could smell the delicious scent of chickens roasting on open spits.

As they descended, Sindbad heaved the great canopy to the left, steering it towards a patch of soft grass below the palace walls.

Just before they touched down, however, a ferocious wind hurled them up into the air once again. It didn't seem to affect any other object, as though it had been aimed at them, and them alone.

Wailing with terror as they were thrust up into the sky, the four travellers clung hold of the ropes with all their might, trailing against the headwind.

At what seemed like lightning speed, they flew for hours, until their limbs were blue and numb with cold.

Clutching hold for dear life, all Scheherazade could think of was the story's seed, and how she'd been so close, but was suddenly so far. In a single fleeting fragment of time, she and Aladdin caught eye contact. Against the hurly-burly of the pulverizing wind, Aladdin seemed to smile reassuringly at the queen.

Through days and nights they flew, stars glinting in the heavens like jewels, and the sun blazing down with all its might. They crossed oceans and landmasses, immeasurable and bleak.

Then, all of a sudden, the wind ceased, and they floated down towards the radiant waters of a sea.

Sindbad was the only one enlivened at the sight of waves.

'Breakers!' he cried out in delight.

'We'll drown!' Aladdin gasped in horror.

Once again, the sailor steered the canopy, heaving it to the side with all his strength, guiding it towards a smattering of russet-brown islands, a little archipelago.

This time, there was no sudden wind. And, to their delight, they came to rest on a beach.

One by one, they gave thanks, and congratulated Sindbad.

He stepped forward to the queen, his expression sombre.

'We will get to the City of Brass, and will find the seed,' he said. 'I promise you.'

Scheherazade managed the faintest smile, as though not to grace her lips with it would have been heartless.

'On behalf of all the women whose lives you are saving by helping me, I thank you,' she said.

Twenty-three

APPARENTLY UNFAZED BY the setback, Sindbad marched into the forest bordering the beach, and set to work chopping down a copse of balsa trees.

Ali Baba did what he could to assist, even though he had no experience in building rafts.

'How will we ever find out where we are?' he whined.

'Irrelevant!' the sailor responded.

'Is it?'

'Yes! What matters is where our destination lies.'

'But how will we find it? How will we find the City of Brass?'

Sindbad paused from hacking with his sword.

'The same way any sailor ever reaches where they want to go.'

'How?'

'By asking the wind to take us,' he said.

At that moment, the queen approached.

'I am going into the forest to search for fruit,' she explained.

The sailor frowned.

'Better for me to go with you,' he retorted. 'It's not safe for a woman.'

Pacing forward to where Sindbad was standing, sword in his fist, Scheherazade raised her hand and slapped him across his cheek.

'Never again doubt the ability of a woman,' she snapped. 'Especially one who's a queen.'

Calling Aladdin to join her, the two of them set off into the hinterland.

Twenty-four

AT THE WESTERN edge of the archipelago, the island was rimmed with beaches that gave way to forest, and the forest to crumbling outcrops of rock at its core.

With no signs of human life whatsoever, nature had taken an unyielding hold, or at least something had, whether it was natural or not.

As they picked their way through the undergrowth, climbing over roots and pushing away vines, Scheherazade and Aladdin noticed the lack of birds and other creatures. It was as if every possible form of life had been scared away.

'D'you feel it?' Aladdin asked, as they tramped ahead.

'Yes I do,' Scheherazade answered right away, even before hearing what 'it' was. 'But we can't set sail on Sindbad's craft until we've gathered a good supply of food.'

Just then, they spotted a magnificent dragonfly coursing through the forest, a kaleidoscope of light playing over its rainbow wings. Without thinking, both women hurried after it, as though hoping it might lead them to a secret.

And that's exactly what it did.

Pausing to drink from the sap of a towering tree, the creature shot upwards into the boughs.

'Look! There!' cried Scheherazade, pointing.

'Breadfruit!'

Aladdin scaled the tree, and started throwing down the enormous prickly fruits.

Taking shelter from the bombardment, Scheherazade

stepped back into the surrounding undergrowth. To her surprise, she spotted another rainbow dragonfly skimming through the leaves. Again, she felt drawn to it, and took chase before realizing what she was doing.

A short distance from the breadfruit tree, into the boughs of which Aladdin had climbed, Scheherazade came to a tree covered in perfectly ripe plums. Plucking one, she bit into it, and was overwhelmed at the delicious taste.

Reaching up for another, she was caught off-balance.

She lurched backwards, arms flailing left and right.

As she tumbled to the ground, her sandal slipped from her foot. She peered around to see where it had gone, and realized it had fallen down a hole.

On hands and knees, she looked down into it.

What had at first appeared to be no more than a little pit was in actual fact a shaft, the width of a barrel.

Straining to focus in the darkness, she saw something glinting and gleaming far below. Overcome with curiosity, Scheherazade was unable to help herself. Taking hold of a good-sized vine from a nearby tree, she unfurled it, and used it to climb down.

Within a few minutes she was standing on the shaft's floor, and saw her sandal had become lodged in the branches of a tree that grew from its base. As she reached up to retrieve her shoe, her gaze was diverted to something extraordinary.

In the lower branches, an oval mirror was hanging, as though positioned with care to provide illumination. But it wasn't the mirror that amazed the queen. Rather, it was the fact that among the branches was a kingdom of miniature people, none of them taller than a man's thumb.

Their skin was painted in vivid colours, and they were dressed in costumes fabricated from the bark of the tree. They appeared to live in little houses fixed to the branches, and were climbing up and down tiny ladders as they went about their lives.

Remarkably, none of the little people had noticed Scheherazade. Watching them for a good long while, she took in the details of the civilization, marvelling at it.

All of a sudden she heard a squeaking, and saw an especially small figure, a little boy, pointing up at her. He was screaming out, warning all the others that an attack was about to take place.

Instantly, the tiny people hurried into their houses, leaving the tree silent.

'I'm not going to harm you,' Scheherazade said.

Still silence.

'Please don't be afraid,' the queen whispered gently. 'I merely climbed down to get my sandal, which had tumbled down into this hole.'

A little time passed, and the child who'd spotted the visitor in the first place appeared on a slender branch. He'd slunk out of his family's house, and didn't seem to have any fear at all.

'If you try and kill us, we'll gobble you up!' he yelled.

A high-pitched squeal followed, as the boy's mother tore out of a house, grabbed him by the scruff of the neck, and dragged him back inside.

Again, Scheherazade spoke:

'I'm not here to harm you,' she said. 'Please come out and let me see you all.'

A few minutes slipped by, then an elderly man stuck his head out from a treehouse.

'Where are you from?' he enquired.

'From beyond the oceans and the mountains,' the queen replied.

Another head appeared – that of a young woman. She asked:

'Did you see the gollop?'

'What's that?'

Pressing her ear close to the tree so she could hear the voices, Scheherazade heard expressions of fear. All of a sudden, everyone was out of their homes, waving their fists.

'The gollop wants to eat us!' yelled the woman.

'If he gets us, he'll chew us up!' exclaimed another.

'We live in terror of him!' howled an old lady, no taller than a toothpick.

'I felt a coldness up in the forest,' Scheherazade answered. 'As though there was something lurking there, something keeping creatures away.'

'The gollop!' the miniature people cried, their voice as one.

'Who are you?' the queen asked.

'We're Grilliax.'

'Are there more of you?'

'There used to be,' a young man said. 'But one by one all the villages like ours were devoured by the gollop. So we're the last one.'

Scheherazade scratched a fingertip to her cheek.

'Is there any way of stopping the gollop?' she asked.

The villagers all spoke at once.

'I can't understand you! You'll have to speak one at a time.'

The young man pushed to the front.

'There's only one way to stop the gollop,' he cried.

'What's that?'

'By catching him in a net, and throwing him into the sea.'

'I wish I could help you,' Scheherazade replied, 'but as soon as we've built a raft, we will leave the island.'

The voices all cried out again:

'Before you go, please catch the gollop for us!'

'But I don't even know what the gollop looks like,' the queen said. 'And I don't have a net.'

'We can help,' said the little boy, shimmying up a branch no thicker than a twig. Fumbling, he pulled out a tiny scroll, and unfurled it.

Scheherazade took in a neat drawing of a creature with whiskers, pointed ears, arched back, and long tail.

'That's a cat,' she said with certainty.

'It's a *gollop*!' the tiny people replied.

'It may be a gollop to you, but to me it's a cat, and I know how to catch cats.'

'With a net!' the people yelled. 'You'll need a net!'

'No need for a net.'

'What will you use if not a net?'

'A fish,' said Scheherazade.

Twenty-five

CLIMBING BACK OUT of the hole, the queen promised to return once the gollop had been caught.

Then, heaving the breadfruits back to the beach with Aladdin, she found the raft almost complete. Sindbad had stripped a dozen balsa trees of their bark, and bolted the trunks together with nails fashioned from palm wood. As for a sail, he'd made it from Baibar's shirt.

The breadfruits were loaded aboard, along with a supply of coconuts filled with water.

'Sindbad,' Scheherazade said, 'can you catch me a fish?'

Before she knew it, the sailor had caught a huge tuna, and had roasted it on the beach. Cutting off the tail, she disappeared into the forest once again.

An hour later, she emerged with an exceedingly affectionate tabby cat, purring in her arms.

'Where did that come from?' Ali Baba asked.

'From the forest. Apparently she's the only cat on the island.'

Handing the animal to Ali Baba, she headed into the forest again.

'I'll be back soon,' she said.

Retracing her steps to where the breadfruit tree stood, Scheherazade climbed down into the shaft, and addressed the Grilliax.

'Did you see the gollop?' they asked fretfully, their tiny faces gripped with fear.

'Yes.'

'Did you manage to catch it?'

The queen nodded.

'Yes I did. And, there's no need to throw it into the sea.'

'Then what will you do with the terrible gollop?' yelled the little boy.

'I'll take her with us and release her on an island much larger than this.'

The villagers cooed with delight.

'How can we ever thank you?'

'No thanks are needed,' replied Scheherazade.

A round of applause went up.

'Now, I must leave,' said the queen.

'Wait!' yelled one of the women.

'We have something for you!' a second cried out.

'A sacred relic!' called a third.

All together, they dragged a circular object over, which was hanging on the end of a branch.

'It fell from the sky!' the first woman hollered.

'From the home of the gods!' bawled the second.

'It'll make your wishes come true!' the third shouted.

Taking the object with thanks, Scheherazade recognized it as a twist of wire, dropped perhaps by a passing bird.

'I'll wear it always,' she said, slipping it onto her finger as a ring.

Twenty-six

THE RAFT SET sail at first light, laden with coconuts, breadfruit, and with the tabby cat as an extra passenger.

Although uncertain of which direction to take, Sindbad the Sailor followed his nose, and asked the wind to guide the way. At times he may have been self-important and haughty, but the others marvelled at him. As incompetent as he'd been riding a horse, he was in his element before the mast.

Tilting out of the water, the raft skimmed along at a tearing pace. All day it kept on a heading due west. As night cloaked the waves and revealed heavens glinting above, Sindbad lowered the sail fashioned from the Black Jinn's shirt.

Through the light of six days they sailed, catching fish when they could, to the delight of the gollop, which made a change from the diet of breadfruit. And through the darkness of six nights, the vast nocturnal firmament above awed each one of the travellers, reminding them of their insignificance.

Each evening, one of them would tell a tale for the amusement of the others.

One night, the gollop cradled in her arms, Aladdin offered to recount an adventure.

'Each one of you has lived far more interesting lives than me,' she said. 'So forgive me if what I say is not worthy of your ears. This is what I have to tell...'

Casting her head back, drinking in a hundred billion stars, she stroked a hand tenderly over the tabby's back, and began:

Once upon a time, in the distant reaches of Hind, there lived a king who had everything a man could ever wish for. His stables were filled with the finest horses, his treasure vaults piled with gold and jewels, and in his apartments there were the most lovely women ever to have graced the earth.

But, as is the way of men, the ruler – whom we shall call King Shalimar – was not content. Rather, the more material wealth he gained, and the more radiant the women who attended him, the less content he became. Through long days and nights, he called for larger and larger platters of food to be brought so that sweetmeats could take his mind off his state of melancholy.

There were platters of shish kebabs laid out on beds of rice, entire roast sheep, sides of beef, and melons the size of cannonballs. Day and night the king gorged himself, until he was the size of an ox. Eventually, he became so fat that he could hardly get out of bed.

Moaning and groaning, he promised to bury in a heap of gold anyone who could cure his sorrowful state. As you can imagine, everyone in the kingdom grew very excited.

Queuing up in a zigzagging line that snaked through the capital's streets, they tried to cure the king's state of melancholy one by one. Some people told jokes. Others jumped up and down and spun around. One or two inflated camels' bladders and popped them.

But nothing worked. The king was more despondent than ever. The chief vizier was about to dispatch a messenger to the neighbouring kingdom to plead for help when he heard a disturbance at the palace gates. A young boy was being scolded by the royal guard. The vizier came to learn that the boy wanted to make the king happy again, as was his right.

'Everyone else who's tried has failed,' the vizier said sternly. 'What makes you think you're any different?'

'I'm different because I don't think like the adults,' the boy answered. 'I think like a child.'

'And is that good?' asked the vizier.

A sparkle in his eye, the little boy broke into a grin.

'Of course it is,' he answered, 'because it's how people are supposed to think!'

The boy was cleaned up, instructed in how to behave in front of the monarch, and led into the royal chamber. Making his way to the bed, he bowed, then said:

'Your Majesty, I haven't come to cure you so much as to tell you something. I'm afraid to say that you'll drop dead within a month, because an assassin has been sent to kill you.'

The ruler, who was lying back on a pile of pillows, munching at a platter of kebabs, looked up in horror.

'How do you know this?!' he exclaimed.

'I know it because my father works in a distant kingdom, and he overheard the assassin telling another that he's coming for you.'

The king was about to call the guards when the boy stopped him.

'There's nothing you can do to halt the assassin,' he said.

'Of course I can, because I have a thousand guards protecting me!'

'No, no, no,' the boy replied. 'You see, the assassin that's coming for you is wearing a magic cloak which makes him invisible.'

The king's forehead furrowed like a farmer's field. Pushing away the kebabs, he clambered out of bed and started pacing up and down.

'Your Majesty,' said the boy, 'I have to leave now, but if you are still alive in a month, I shall return.'

The boy left the palace. With him gone, the king paced up and down day and night, ceasing only to sleep a few minutes from time to time, or to answer the call of nature.

All he could think about was the assassin

in the cloak of invisibility, and how he might gain entrance into the royal apartment.

Unable to eat even a single grape through worry, the king paced on and on, his mind racing. On strict orders, no one was admitted into the royal bedchamber, for fear the assassin would slip in at the same time.

Precisely a month after his first visit, the boy returned to the palace. Given the king's panicky state, even he wasn't permitted entrance. Eventually, he managed to climb in through the window.

The king screamed.

'You've come to kill me!' he roared.

'No I have not,' the boy replied. 'If you remember, it was me who told you about the assassin. And, if you look at me, you'll see that I'm not wearing a cloak of invisibility.'

'Well,' the ruler stammered, 'if you look at me, you will see I'm still very much alive!'

'Yes,' the boy replied, 'and if you walk to the mirror over there, you will see that you are half the weight you were a month ago.'

'I didn't eat,' the king moaned. 'I was too fearful.'

The boy grinned from ear to ear.

'Now that I've cured your case of overeating,' he said, 'I shall take you into the mountains with me.'

'Why would I ever agree to that?' the king demanded petulantly.

'Because, you may think you have absolutely everything, but there's one thing you don't have,' he said.

'And what might that be?'

'A friend,' said the boy.

And so, the king and the boy went into the mountains together and became firm friends. The king offered to have the child buried in gold pieces, but the boy asked for the reward to be given to the poor.

When asked why, he answered:

'Because I've seen the sadness of money, and the joy of freedom.'

And, I am pleased to say that the king was never sorrowful again, and the little boy always had a sparkle in his eye, even when he grew into a man.

Twenty-seven

A WEEK AFTER leaving the island, the winds failed, and the raft was becalmed.

Sindbad tried with all his might pick up the airstream, but with no luck. Day after day, the travellers and the cat sprawled out on the raft, each one dreaming of being far away.

'It's surely a curse,' Sindbad moaned.

'We'll die here,' Ali Baba added gloomily.

'I wish we'd never left the island,' Aladdin griped.

Scheherazade wasn't listening. She was gazing at something between the horizon and the raft.

'D'you see that?' she asked curiously.

The others looked around, and found themselves focussing on a mountainous wave approaching them.

Sindbad, Ali Baba, and Aladdin let out a cry of horror.

A colossal wave of dark blue water surged ahead, as if it was aiming at them. Leaning over into the sea, the travellers tried to paddle out of the way, but there was no hope.

The water swept forwards, gathering speed, breakers cresting in foamy white waves.

Just before the raft was crushed into matchwood, something happened that bewildered all four passengers, and the gollop as well.

The vast mountain of water dredged from the deep halted in its tracks.

A pair of uneven horns pushed up to the surface, and

then a giant head – a head with a single blinking eye and a delighted, smiling mouth.

'Baibar!' the travellers all cried, cheering at the top of their lungs.

The Black Jinn emerged from the water, his body strewn with seaweed.

'How ever did you find us?' Scheherazade exclaimed.

'By swimming through all the oceans of the world,' Baibar answered. 'I knew I'd find you eventually.' He frowned. 'Where are you going?'

Sindbad the Sailor cursed.

'Nowhere!' he cried. 'We've been becalmed.'

'Then I'll pull you behind me as I swim.'

The queen looked at the jinn.

'D'you know the way to the City of Brass?' she yelled.

Nodding, Baibar pointed to the horizon.

Scheherazade smiled, then sighed, the tabby cat nestled on her lap.

'I promised the Grilliax people we'd take this gollop to an island much larger than their own.'

'Isn't that a cat?' the Black Jinn asked, confused.

'Yes,' the queen responded firmly, 'but it's a gollop as well.'

The jinn winked.

'I passed a fine island on the way here. We could stop there,' he said.

And that was what they did.

Twenty-eight

PULLING THE RAFT over the horizon, and then across the next, the Black Jinn towed it into the bay of a large island, the harbour walled in battlements.

The travellers clambered ashore, each of them thrilled at standing once again on solid ground. Right away, Sindbad set about checking the sail, while Aladdin and Ali Baba went in search of supplies and fresh water.

The tabby cat in her arms, Scheherazade spoke to the Black Jinn:

'We don't want to scare people,' she said, 'so it may be better for you to disguise yourself.'

Baibar shrugged.

'Do you have any particular form in mind?'

'Something a little less conspicuous than what you are.'

Turning around, the queen found a beautiful young woman standing on the quay. Smiling, the queen spoke a greeting, and asked the name of the island.

'I don't know,' the woman answered. 'It's *me*, Baibar!'

Scheherazade winced.

'Didn't recognize you!'

The Black Jinn cackled.

'I don't know how you get used to being so small, and why you think you need two eyes instead of one.'

'You get used to it,' Scheherazade said.

Together, they walked the short distance from the port into the town to find someone who might adopt the gollop.

As they strolled through the streets, people peered down from their windows.

Baibar rubbed a hand over his head.

'Can you check I don't still have my horns?' he whispered.

'No sign of them. Why d'you ask?'

'Haven't you noticed?'

'Noticed what?'

'Everyone's looking at us in a strange way.'

The queen glanced up, and saw faces clustered at the windows – the faces of concerned men looking down.

'There aren't any women,' Scheherazade said.

'How could that be?'

At that moment, a voice called out from the shadow of a doorway.

Pausing, the two strangers went over.

'What are you doing?!' exclaimed a wizened old man, standing at the front of his carpentry shop.

'We're looking for someone to take this gollop. I mean, this cat,' said the queen.

The local balked.

'No,' he said frostily. 'What I mean is – what are you two women doing in the street?'

In his best pretty-young-woman voice, Baibar answered:

'As my friend told you, we are looking for a home for this cat.'

The old carpenter shook his head in consternation.

'You'll be rounded up by the guard and forced to toil in the mines.'

'Mines? What mines?' asked the queen.

'The opal mines... in which all the women are kept prisoner.'

Scheherazade's back warmed with anger.

'And who on earth would force the women to work in the mines?'

'King Artal, of course.'

'For what reason?'

'Revenge, for the fact that his wife laughed at him in public.'

'For that, he imprisoned *all* women?' Baibar asked.

The ancient nodded.

'My own wife, daughters, and granddaughters are kept prisoner there,' he explained glumly.

A mask of rage descended over Scheherazade's face.

Smiling demurely, she addressed the old man:

'Do you like cats?'

A moment later, the gollop had been thrust into the carpenter's arms, and the two strangers were hurrying back to the port.

'We're ready to go!' Sindbad called hastily. 'Next stop, the City of Brass!'

'*No*,' Scheherazade replied. 'Even though time's against us, we can't leave yet.'

The sailor shrugged.

'Why not?'

'Because it seems as though my husband, King Shahriyar, isn't the only tyrant who needs to be taught a lesson.'

Still disguised as the young woman, the Black Jinn bristled.

'I'll pull off his head and squash it like a ripe grape!'

Sindbad and Ali Baba regarded the young woman in horror.

'Who's she?' Aladdin hissed under her breath.

The jinn grinned boisterously.

'It's *me*, it's Baibar!' he cried.

Twenty-nine

SCHEHERAZADE SENT THE others into the town to learn what they could about King Artal.

She suggested the Black Jinn transform himself into the guise of a young man. He'd done so even before the request had been made. The queen herself tied back her hair, donned a heavy robe, and rubbed soot into her cheeks.

By the evening, her fellow travellers were back at the harbour.

'They say the king loves mechanical objects,' Aladdin reported.

'And that he's holding a competition for the finest machine,' Sindbad added.

'And,' Ali Baba said, 'whoever wins the competition will be allowed to ask any favour they wish of the king.'

Scheherazade clasped her hands together.

'We'll build an amazing machine and win the competition!' she snapped.

The Black Jinn's eyes glinted.

There was a flash of light.

A mechanical juggler appeared on the quayside, and began throwing juggling clubs high into the air, and catching them.

The queen barked at Baibar, ordering him to get rid of the object.

'No magic!' she exclaimed for the thousandth time.

Aladdin stepped forward.

'If we're to build a machine,' she said, 'what shall it be?'

They all thought for a long time, except the Black Jinn, who wasn't permitted to submit ideas.

'A musical box,' Ali Baba said.

'A calculating machine,' Sindbad suggested.

'What about a digging machine?' mumbled Aladdin.

'*Yes*!' Scheherazade exclaimed. 'A digging machine!'

Working together, the four travellers designed a mechanism that would burrow into the ground while playing music at the same time.

The carpenter who'd taken the gollop allowed them a space at the back of his workshop, and provided scraps of wood. At first, the thought of constructing a machine was perplexing, after all, none of the travellers was an engineer.

But, discussing the problem at hand, each one realized they could help in the design.

Ali Baba remembered marvelling at a waterwheel on a river near Baghdad.

Aladdin sketched a system of gears she'd seen at the port of Alexandria, linking a winch to a counterweight.

And Sindbad described a coiled spring he'd heard of on a voyage to Cathay, said to power the emperor's fleet of dragon ships.

Having listened to the suggestions, Scheherazade thought of how, as a child, she'd spent time in the palace workshops, as her father was a friend of the chief inventor. Closing her eyes, she remembered the engineer drawing mechanisms, and explaining to her how machinery worked.

Out of all the appliances created there, the most alluring had been a model ship. Powered by steam, and with a full set of gears, it had zigzagged over the royal lake, playing music as it went.

While the others milled about, the queen drew the outline of the digging machine. Then, taking fresh sheets of paper, she sketched the intricate workings – gears, boilers, springs, and scoops.

Once she was finished, they all got to work making the pieces from bronze, iron, and wood.

Thirty

AT THE PALACE gates, a special guard inspected each machine as it arrived, checking and double-checking it wasn't a weapon with which to bring down the monarchy.

A line of fearful engineers made their way into the throne room, dressed in their best clothes, and pushing their machines. There were great water-clocks, and devices that could mimic the sound of jungle birds; automatons that seemed utterly lifelike, and even contraptions that could enable an ordinary man to breathe underwater.

Sitting on his throne, King Artal had an immense golden crown heavy on his head.

One at a time, the devices were presented to the monarch, who seemed completely uninterested, as if he'd seen it all before – which he had.

As soon as one of the machines was pushed forward, he would wave a hand angrily – a signal for the contrivance and its engineer to be taken to the back door and thrown out.

The digging machine was the very last contraption to be pushed into the hall. Being as large as it was, extra guards were called to inspect it carefully.

The king watched, his curiosity piqued, as not one, but five engineers attended the device, which had trundled forward under its own power.

'And what is the use of this ridiculous apparatus?' he asked his vizier.

The official exchanged words with Scheherazade, still disguised as a man.

'We call it "The Liberator",' she announced in a deep voice.

King Artal let out a scornful squeal.

'Pray tell, what is it designed to liberate?'

'Perhaps Your Majesty would allow my associate to demonstrate.'

The king waved a hand to the side, indicating that a quick demonstration was in order.

Still in the guise of a strapping young man, Baibar strode over and turned a mechanical key until the spring was coiled as tight as it would go.

Aladdin opened a series of valves on the underside.

Ali Baba jerked an iron lever to the left.

Climbing into the seat, Sindbad strapped himself in.

He glanced at Scheherazade, who nodded.

The machine fired into life, sparks flying, trumpets blaring full blast. As the monarch's eyes widened in horror, the mechanism dug down through the throne room's floor.

Within ten minutes, Sindbad had burrowed straight down, and then through reinforced rock walls to the mines, in which all the women of the kingdom were forced to toil.

Like a monster from the furthest limits of a child's imagination, the digging machine reversed, leading the enslaved women up into the throne room.

The tunnelling had knocked the king's crown off his head, and him off the throne. He was being comforted by his courtiers as the contraption surfaced, trumpets blaring like ghouls.

He screeched orders for the device and its engineers to be rounded up and thrown into the dungeons, but such was the noise and pandemonium that no one heard his demands.

Charging out of the tunnel, the mothers, grandmothers, sisters, daughters and aunts fought away the retinue of courtiers, viziers, and hangers-on.

Encircling King Artal, who was huddled on the floor with the royal crown clasped desperately to his chest, they closed in, snarling with rage.

As they did so, a tall, elegant woman approached, the others parting to allow her through.

The monarch's head lowered in trepidation at setting eyes on his consort.

'Forgive me my dear!' he bellowed, afraid that reprisals were on their way.

The queen regarded her husband with repulsion. As she did so, Scheherazade stepped forward, removed her disguise, and introduced herself.

'What shall we do with him?' Queen Artal asked, her tone ice cold.

'I have an idea,' Scheherazade replied brightly.

Pacing over to where the machine was cooling, Sindbad the Sailor still at the controls, the queen explained what to do.

A moment later, the digger was rumbling out of the palace, through the streets, before coming to a halt in the town's great square.

Everyone followed it, including the king. Tied up, he was carried out at shoulder height.

When everyone was standing back, Baibar stepped forward and wound the clock spring again. Then, Aladdin pulled a lever, and Sindbad angled the contraption into the ground.

Like a hot thimble pressed into butter, the digger bored a path straight down into the earth. A moment or two later, it was so deep that no trace of the machine remained.

Throwing the device into reverse, Sindbad the Sailor drove it out.

'Perfect!' cried Scheherazade.

A rope was tied around the king's waist, and he was lowered into the shaft, grunting and groaning as he went.

Then a telescope was sent down, so the deposed monarch could get glimpses of his people, as they peered down, jeering at him, and tossing down rotten fruit.

As celebrations continued throughout the kingdom, Queen Artal assumed the throne. Thanking Scheherazade and her companions, she said:

'As my husband is unavailable to award the prize for the best machine, I shall be the judge. And I have decided that your digging contraption, which saved the kingdom's women, is the clear winner! So, please go ahead and ask your favour, and it will be granted.'

Scheherazade exchanged a glance with Sindbad, Aladdin, Ali Baba, and Baibar.

'Thank you, Your Majesty, but there is nothing we need. We must be leaving the island on the raft on which we arrived.'

The queen clicked her fingers, and spoke into the ear of her chief adviser, her best friend since childhood. Bidding their farewells, the travellers strolled down to the port, the royal guard leading the way.

But the raft made by Sindbad's hands was not standing where it ought to have been. In its place was a magnificent sloop, laden with provisions, its blinding white sail awaiting the breeze.

Ushered aboard by Queen Artal herself, the travellers gave thanks, and set off in the direction of the City of Brass.

Baibar transformed himself back into the Black Jinn that he was, and towed the vessel by brute force towards the setting sun.

Thirty-one

THROUGHOUT THE VOYAGE, Scheherazade fretted that Yunan would see them coming and block their path a second time.

As if reading her thoughts, Aladdin did her best to offer reassurance.

'We *will* succeed,' she said, her voice as solid as stone.

'But even if we evade the sorcerer's spells,' the queen replied, 'we'll be too late to retrieve the story's seed.'

Again, Aladdin offered comfort.

'The journey has strengthened us,' she said, 'preparing us for whatever we face.'

At the end of the day under sail, the sloop glided to a halt, as Baibar waded through the water.

'I must leave you now,' he said.

'Where are you going?' Sindbad shouted. 'We need you to pull us.'

The Black Jinn held up one of his four paws as though pledging a vow.

'I shall be back before the dawn breaks over the horizon,' he said.

And, with that, he was gone.

The four travellers prepared a meal and feasted, then sat back and watched the heavens, as they were in the habit of doing. No matter how great their trials and tribulations, a single glance up at the nocturnal firmament dashed only those problems that were themselves as weighty as the world.

Despite staring long and hard at the billions of specks glinting above, the queen was consumed with worry.

'If you would allow me,' she said, 'I would like to tell you a tale to divert my mind from its troubled state. It's a story my father told me when I was a child – one which is a part of me as much as I am a part of it.'

The others clustered around, eyes trained up at the stars, ears honed to the sound of Scheherazade's voice:

Once upon a time there lived a merchant called Hassan, who was wealthy and generous, happy and fortunate.

But one day, disaster stared him in the face.

His ships, bearing great loads of treasure from afar, were captured by pirates, and his warehouse – containing many valuables – was burned to the ground. Unable to face his friends, he sold his last belongings, and set off in search of his fortune.

But good luck had deserted Hassan. While he was asleep in a caravanserai, a thief stole his remaining money, and this time he found himself without a single coin to his name, and in a strange town.

Ashamed of himself, he went to the mosque-keeper, and asked for alms to see him on his way. How was he ever to hold his head up again, he wondered.

He asked the mosque-keeper what he should do.

'My brother,' said the old man, 'go three days' march from here, and you will arrive at such and such a place. The king there is generous and kind. You may be able to put your case before him, and ask help of a more substantial nature than that which I am able to present you with from our limited resources.'

With these words, he gave Hassan a handful of coins from the poor-box.

Thanking him, Hassan set off, after buying a few dates to eat on the journey. The way was rough, and Hassan was tired, thirsty and dusty by the time he arrived at the walled town.

The shop-keepers there were richly clad and contented of mind. Hassan walked wearily towards the palace, where the old mosque-keeper had told him a generous king fed hundreds of people each night. But when he finally got there he was so ashamed of his rags, and so fearful of presenting himself to the monarch in such a state, that he hid behind a pillar. From that vantage point he peered in awe upon the scene.

Before him, a great concourse of people, young and old, were being presented with food and money by the generous monarch, who sat upon a golden throne in the middle of the lofty hall.

Suddenly, from his hiding place, Hassan spied three magnificent hounds being led out to a spot a few feet away from him. An attendant placed three bowls of the finest meat before each of the dogs. The man then went away, and Hassan found his eyes fixed upon the delicious meat which had been given to the hounds.

As he was thinking that he could feed from the leavings of the animals, so great was his hunger, the dog nearest to him raised its eyes to his, and – looking at him in an almost human fashion – pushed its jewelled golden bowl towards Hassan.

The famished man, unable to wait a second longer, helped himself to one of the pieces of meat, and pushed the bowl back to the dog. But, with its paw, the animal again nudged it over to Hassan, until he had eaten to his heart's content. Then the creature ate, and after it had licked the bowl clean, it shoved it back towards Hassan.

The man saw that it was offering him the bowl, and when he took it in his hands and then hid the precious object under his tattered cloak, the animal seemed to nod its head in agreement.

Hassan realized that if he sold the bowl, and bought himself new clothes, he would at least have a chance to approach a merchant for some sort of work.

Patting the hound gratefully on the head, he slipped away from the crowd. Next day, he sold the bowl. Being studded with precious jewels, it brought such a good price that he was able to set up in business for himself.

By shrewd trading, soon he had enough merchandise to take back to his native town, where his friends greeted him with much joy.

Good luck having returned, Hassan became a successful trader, and before long was once again as rich as he had ever been.

Some years later, he felt the urge to return to the town where he'd been shown such kindness by the dog, and he made up his mind to replace the golden food bowl which the hound had lent him.

Within a few days a replica of the bowl was ready, and Hassan, on his best horse, with flowing robes and boots of the finest leather, set off.

At last he arrived, and once more saw the old wall which was built around the town. But upon riding inside the gates, he saw with amazement that the glory of the palace was no more. The building lay wide open to the sky, roofless and ruined, its beautiful pillars broken as if destroyed by Mongol hordes.

All around, the wrecked houses were silent and empty, the shops where rich and contented merchants had sat were despoiled of all their merchandise, and there seemed to be no living thing in the whole place.

Sorrowfully, Hassan began mounting his horse to ride away, when a great hound darted out of the palace ruins, followed by two others. Hassan recognized them as the handsome dogs that had been brought by the attendant to feed from the golden bowls, when he was a beggar in that very place.

Then an old man appeared, in a rough woollen robe and with a stick in his hand, upon which he leant heavily.

'Greetings, my son,' said the man. 'What brings you to this place?'

'Some time ago I came here in rags,' Hassan explained, 'and was fortunate enough to be given the meat from a bowl by this dog here. When I left I took the bowl, sold it, and replenished my fortunes, and now I've come to repay the debt, and provide this replica of the golden bowl.'

'Those times are long gone,' said the old man. 'As you will have noticed, the vanity and pomp which was once my court has vanished.'

Hassan grasped that he was speaking to the generous king whom, long before, he had seen feeding the poor and needy in the great palace.

'Your Majesty,' said he, 'please take this golden bowl which I have brought.'

'No,' said the old king, 'I have no need for anything, except that which I have here. My dogs catch game for my one daily meal, and a gardener has remained with me, and continues to grow a few vegetables in ground that was once the palace gardens. Together, he, the hounds, and I manage to enjoy our lives. After our enemies destroyed the kingdom, and my people were taken as slaves, we have lived simply here.'

'But, but, the bowl, the golden bowl,' whispered Hassan. 'May I not leave it for Your Majesty?'

'If a dog of mine thought fit to give away his bowl,' said the king, 'it is not for me to take it back. I am sure that he has no need of it now. Go, return from whence you came, we are provided for.'

Bowing to the king, Hassan mounted his horse and rode away. Glancing back, he saw the old king leaning upon his stick, waving a last farewell, the hounds at his feet.

In the days and years that followed, Hassan

often told the story, that men should not forget the tale...

...of The King, the Dog, and the Golden Bowl.

Thirty-two

THE BLACK JINN emerged from the waves as the sun broke over the horizon.

A horrifying gash covered his right cheek, and his single eye was bloodshot, as though a terrible catastrophe had befallen him during the night.

While the others clustered around, Scheherazade asked tenderly what had happened.

'A matter of honour,' Baibar answered.

'How was it that you, the mighty Black Jinn, could be vanquished?' Ali Baba called.

The jinn struggled half a smile.

'*I* was the victor,' he said.

Taking the rope in his paw, he began towing the ship towards the distance, but so weakened was he that progress was slow.

At Sindbad's suggestion, the jinn transformed himself into a passenger and rode with the others, while the sloop picked up the wind.

By day and by night, a thousand miles of water was covered. Through every inch of the journey, Scheherazade fretted about the mission. And, as the days passed, Baibar's wounds healed, and he began to regain his strength.

By the time land was sighted, none of the travellers could remember how long they'd been aboard. All they knew was that time was against them, and that by not trying, there was no hope at all of success.

The first sight of the city's outline was spellbinding, as though it had been painted with an artist's brush. Sindbad pointed at the skyline, a hundred brass domes glinting in the early evening light.

One at a time, the others sat up and stared at it, each awestruck.

Aladdin gasped in wonder.

Ali Baba let out a resounding whoop of joy.

Scheherazade said nothing. She merely stood on the deck, gazing in gladness, tears rolling down her cheeks.

Beside her, in the guise of a young man, the Black Jinn smiled to himself.

'We must prepare our defences,' the queen said, as the sloop docked at the harbour. 'Or else we'll be carried away to the ends of the earth for a second time.'

'We shall not meet opposition,' Baibar said, as they climbed onto the quay.

The others looked at him.

'What do you know that we do not?' Sindbad asked.

The Black Jinn, or rather the young man, blushed.

'Only that Yunan the sorcerer recently met with an unfortunate accident,' he said. 'So I would be very surprised if he caused any mischief here, or anywhere else.'

Aladdin was the next to speak:

'Where will we find the story's seed?' she asked.

All eyes moved to Scheherazade.

'I don't know,' she said apologetically.

Ali Baba clapped his hands.

'Let's go and see what information we can gather.'

Dispersing, they spread out into the city, each of them searching alone.

Aladdin found herself in a teahouse below the palace walls.

She asked if anyone had heard of a story's seed. The enquiry was met with shrugs, heads shaking side to side.

'That sounds very unusual,' the owner of the teahouse said. 'And as something unusual, you might expect it to be owned by the king. He has an interest in unusual things, especially unusual things connected to unusual stories.'

Ali Baba took himself to the main square, where a storyteller had just recounted the final verse of his evening's tale.

'Do you know where I might find the seed of a story?' he asked.

'Which story would that be?' the spinner of sagas asked.

'The one telling the tale of a jealous king, and a queen cleverer and more beautiful than the sun is bright.'

'Sounds like a magical tale,' the storyteller replied. 'I'd like to know it.'

Meanwhile, Sindbad's wanderings brought him to a mill. He found a farmer there, waiting for his wheat to be ground into flour.

'Can you tell me where the seed of a tale would be found?' he enquired.

The farmer seemed confused.

'Every sheaf of wheat has a story to tell,' he responded, 'but not the one you could be searching for.'

Still disguised as a fresh-faced young man, Baibar strode

into a park, and watched as the sun slipped down behind the trees.

As he sat on the grass, touched by the beauty of nature, he heard a family of swallows tweeting, as they nested up for the night. Being a jinn, and so understanding the language of all living creatures, Baibar listened.

The father bird said:

'This morning, when I was searching for sticks, I happened to fly through a very tiny hole in the palace wall.'

'And what did you find there?' asked the mother bird.

'A vast cavern in which the king's treasure was hidden.'

'Gold and jewels, and all the nonsense humans gather for no reason at all?'

'Yes,' the father bird replied. 'All the usual treasure. Except, there was a box that caught my eye. It was a big wooden seed.'

Far more anxious than the others because her life was on the line, Scheherazade zigzagged through the city, asking anyone and everyone she encountered if they'd heard of a story seed.

Assuming her to be a foreigner who was deranged, they smiled politely, and hurried away. Before heading back down to the harbour, where she had planned to meet the others, she spotted a blind beggar feeling his way along a wall.

Sidling up, she gave greeting, and asked if he had ever heard of a story's seed.

'Pray tell, why do you search for such an unlikely object?' he asked.

Scheherazade swallowed hard.

'There was once a girl who married a tyrannical king to save the lives of innocent women – women he would have killed. Each night she told him a story, or rather part of a story. The tale continued for many nights, or at least it was supposed to,' she said. 'But, seeing what the queen was doing, the king's sorcerer set the story on a path of adversity. And the only way the queen can return it to where it ought to be is by finding the seed of the tale from the City of Brass.'

The blind beggar smiled endearingly.

'If it's not too much to ask,' he said, 'tell me what you will do if and when you find the seed.'

Scheherazade's face froze.

'I don't know,' she said. 'All I can hope is that a course of action will reveal itself.'

The beggar gave apologies for not being able to help, but blessed the young woman who'd told her tale. Thanking him, Scheherazade took a coin from the folds of her robe, kissed it, and pressed it into the beggar's hand.

At midnight, the travellers met up at the boat, their expressions downcast.

Only Baibar had news.

'In the king's treasure vault there's a precious object made from a seed,' he said.

Sindbad winced.

'How did you come up with that?'

The Black Jinn looked bashful.

'A little bird told me.'

Scheherazade thanked her companions.

'After all our journeying to the City of Brass, I half-imagined the seed would be waiting for us, served up on a silver platter.'

Ali Baba regarded the queen fondly.

'In my experience,' he mused, 'nothing of value is ever gained with ease.'

'We can break into the king's treasury!' Baibar exclaimed.

Sindbad balked at the suggestion.

'And get slaughtered for our trouble?'

Her mood sullen, the queen suggested they all turn in for the night. She herself sat out on the deck, thinking of all the innocent lives her husband's cruelty had brought to such a needless end. Even if she could end his brutal ways, she'd still be married to him – a fate worse than death.

Thirty-three

EARLY NEXT MORNING, a procession of soldiers wearing the livery of the royal guard marched out from the palace, through the streets, and down to the port.

The first to hear them approaching, Sindbad the Sailor called the alarm.

'We don't stand a chance against them!' Aladdin cried.

'Give me the order and I'll do what I can,' said Baibar.

'Let's find out what they want,' Scheherazade answered.

As his men stood to attention on the quayside, the commander made an announcement:

'Last night, a young woman, who's been traced to this vessel, stopped to talk to a blind beggar on a narrow street,' he said. 'She gave him a silver dinar.'

Baibar and the others stiffened, expecting trouble.

'It was me,' Scheherazade said. 'I met the beggar, and I gave him a coin. If it was against the laws of this country, I am sorry. As a foreigner in the City of Brass, I was unaware of the protocols. And, if there's a charge, it will be me who pays it, and not those who travel with me.'

The commander-in-chief asked Scheherazade to accompany his troops.

'We will not allow her to go without us,' said Aladdin.

'Very well, you may come, too,' the commander said sternly.

A moment later, the travellers were walking at a fast pace through the streets, soldiers marching either side of them. As

127

they approached the palace gates, the great portals opened from within.

In less time than it takes to tell, the five visitors to the City of Brass were standing in the great hall, at the end of which was a simple throne. It wasn't ornate or even especially regal, like the throne of King Artal, or even that of Scheherazade's own husband. Rather, it was carved from teak, and festooned with silk.

Upon the throne was sitting a young man. Unlike the other sovereigns they had met on their adventures, he was surprisingly ordinary. More to the point, though, he seemed contented.

As soon as the visitors arrived, he got to his feet and walked down the hall to greet them.

'My name is Arsalan,' he said. 'And I am the King of the City of Brass.'

The travellers kissed the monarch's hand one at a time.

The king turned to Scheherazade.

'Do you not recognize me?' he asked, a glint in his eye.

'No,' she said, her mind on the story seed. 'No I don't.'

The king smiled broadly.

'Last night you provided a blind beggar a little conversation when he needed it greatly, and a silver coin as well.'

'That is true,' the queen said. 'Is there a law against it in these parts?'

King Arsalan broke into a peal of laughter.

'I shall tell you a secret,' he said. 'It is my habit to quit the palace from time to time and wander the streets of the capital at night, so as to learn the needs of my people. And last night I was dressed in the guise of a blind beggar when you approached me, asking for the seed of a story.'

Scheherazade stepped back in surprise.

'Well, I'm pleased that your luck has changed and your sight has been restored since our last meeting,' she answered with a grin. 'If you will forgive me, I am in an agitated state because I must find the seed of the story.'

The king's gaze feasted reflectively upon the magnificent Shirazi carpet on which he was standing.

'I have something to show you,' he said.

The monarch clapped his hands and a pair of pages shuffled into the throne room. Carried between them was a silken cushion, upon which was a kind of wooden box – a wooden box fashioned from a coco de mer.

'This object has been in the kingdom's treasure vault for a thousand years,' King Arsalan explained. 'The annals of the court record that it was brought to the palace by an elderly woman, who said that one day, a beautiful young queen would come asking for it.' The monarch smiled gently. 'You are a beautiful young woman,' he said, 'but are you a queen?'

Stepping forward, Sindbad the Sailor bowed.

'Your Majesty,' he said, 'the woman who stands before you is none other than Scheherazade, the queen married to an oppressive king named Shahriyar.'

King Arsalan motioned to the coco de mer.

'Then, I believe this treasure is your property, and not mine,' he said.

Expressing her most sincere thanks, the queen stepped forward and took the story's seed.

'May I enquire how you intend to return to your kingdom?' the king asked.

'We will sail there, Your Majesty,' Sindbad called out.

Scheherazade sighed.

'Even if we travel at the pace of a whirlwind,' she said, 'destiny may be against us.'

Again, the monarch glanced down at the floor, his gaze tracing the pattern of the beautiful carpet on which he, and his guests, were standing. He remained silent for several minutes, as though watching events unfold.

'The kingdom of Shahriyar is a hundred horizons from here,' he declared. 'So returning there by conventional means will take months, or even years.'

Scheherazade's eyes welled with tears.

'Then many more innocent women will lose their lives,' she replied.

King Arsalan stepped backwards, until his feet were touching stone. Having whispered a secret incantation entrusted to him as a child, the carpet upon which the travellers were standing floated up into the air.

'This carpet will take you back to the land of King Shahriyar,' he said. 'I wish you good fortune!'

The magnificent Shirazi carpet banked to the left, and flew out of the window of the throne room. Sitting down on the intricate geometric pattern, Scheherazade held the story's seed on her lap. As the carpet flew, her fingers caressed it, as she took in the carved surface.

Far below, the burnished domes of the city glinted like jewels. Soaring up into the clouds, the carpet flew on and on: over jungles and deserts, over mighty mountain ranges and across oceans, until it began descending.

At its own pace, the carpet drifted down and came to a rest at the edge of a forest.

'I know where we are,' Scheherazade said.

Stepping off the carpet, the travellers thanked it for transporting them. One of the corners furled upwards as though waving farewell and, rising up into the heavens, it hastened back whence it had come.

The queen led the others through the forest to a ramshackle home. Even before they arrived at the door, it opened.

Inside, the Blue Witch was waiting.

'I have the seed of the story!' Scheherazade exclaimed, even before giving salutations. 'Look! I have it here, brought from far away.'

The witch greeted the queen and her companions.

'You must hurry!' she cried.

'Where? What shall I do with the seed?'

The Blue Witch paused, her eyes burning into those of the queen. 'You must work out the next steps for yourself,' she said. 'You have the answers. Take them, and save the kingdom from its king!'

Thirty-four

A flash of light blinded Scheherazade and the others, and they found themselves transported to a patch of wasteland, as the dawn light washed the city walls in a blush of pink.

The land was lined with hundreds and hundreds of uniform graves, each one marked with no more than the name of a queen.

A few feet from where they were standing was a fresh grave, yet to be filled. And beyond it were an executioner's block and an axe, the blade as sharp as any.

'This grave is my destination,' said Scheherazade.

'No!' Aladdin snapped. 'Not if we solve the riddle, and work out how to use the seed.'

Ali Baba stepped forward.

'Look at it carefully,' he said.

'It's covered in intricate carvings,' Sindbad added.

'Carvings of an adventure,' Aladdin mused.

'Strange,' Ali Baba said.

'What is?' the queen asked.

'Well, look at the designs and tell me what you see.'

Scheherazade squinted at the relief that covered every inch of the coco de mer.

'I see a group of travellers at a caravanserai, and a desert as great as any, and a jinn billowing up into the sky.'

'And a vast cityscape,' Aladdin added, 'and those look like snake ghouls.'

'And that looks like a sailing sloop on the ocean.'

'That it is,' Ali Baba confirmed.

The queen breathed in deeply, as though she'd seen a story she knew.

'This is *our* story,' she said softly. 'The story of our journey... the journey to find the seed.'

Until that moment, Scheherazade had been so concerned with obtaining the seed and bringing it back to the kingdom, she hadn't given any thought to how to activate it. As she and her companions stood gazing at the object at the edge of the makeshift cemetery, there came the sound of soldiers in the distance.

A moment or two passed, then a unit of the royal guard strode out of the imperial gate, a female prisoner, hooded and chained, in their charge. It seemed that they could not see the visitors, who watched in horror.

A stone's throw from them, the condemned woman was led forward to the block in silence.

An executioner stepped from the shadows, picked up his axe.

The prisoner's hood was tugged off.

Scheherazade gasped.

The condemned woman was none other than herself.

Her hands clutching the seed of the story, her face was masked in fear.

'I must work it out!' she exclaimed, studying the images.

Focussing, she caught a fragment of memory.

Her father was leading her through a maze in the palace grounds.

'Baba, we'll never find our way out!' she moaned.

'If you think like that,' her father said, 'of course we won't. But if you concentrate, and turn what you know over in your head, a key will turn in a lock.'

'But I don't see a key, Baba!' the little girl groaned.

'It's there… just as it always is, if you look for it.'

'How will I see it, Baba?'

'By looking in a different way.'

'What d'you mean?'

'Don't look in an obvious way. Look beyond what your eyes are showing you. Use all your senses.'

Scheherazade remembered how she'd smelled something, something familiar – the delicious aroma of pastries wafting through from the palace kitchens. By following the smell, she'd led her father from the maze.

Slowing her breathing, Scheherazade strained once again to think in a different way.

Closing her eyes, she touched the coco de mer to her nostrils, and then to her ear. After that, she ran her fingertips over its carved form.

In the distance, the prisoner was being forced to her knees.

'*Hurry!*' Sindbad barked, tears welling in his eyes.

But Scheherazade wasn't listening.

In her own time, she touched a thumb to the base of the story's seed. Despite clutching the object on her journey across the world, she hadn't noticed that there was a tiny groove on the underside – a groove into which the tip of her thumb fitted, like a hand in a glove.

As it slipped into place, the top of the seed flipped open, releasing a dial.

In the distance, the executioner was stepping into place, the shaft of the axe balanced between both his hands.

'Don't want to rush you,' Aladdin said anxiously, 'but time is against you.'

Scheherazade's eye glinted.

'When has time ever been in our favour?' she asked.

With those words, she looked over at herself, the executioner raising the axe high above him in the crisp morning air.

Then, swallowing, she watched it fall.

With the blade no more than an inch from her neck, Scheherazade turned the dial.

Instantly, the scene froze – the axe suspended mid-air, as though it had been paused.

The queen's companions gasped, unable to speak.

And then, as though she was certain of what to do, she twisted the dial round and around.

As she did so, events that had taken place only moments before were reversed.

The axe lifted into the air.

The executioner stepped back.

Scheherazade stood up, and the hood was returned to its place.

The royal guard marched backwards towards the palace.

And then, as she turned the dial, the most extraordinary thing of all took place.

One by one, each grave was emptied, its headless body

conveyed back to the block, where it was made whole again as the executioner's blade swept upwards.

And each time, the sequence was the same:

The executioner stepped back and the hood was replaced over the queen's head.

The royal guard marched backwards into the palace, and then the next grave was emptied.

Rotating the dial faster and faster, Scheherazade turned back time, until all the graves were empty, and the wasteland was a meadow once again.

Thirty-five

BAIBAR FELL TO his knees, those of a young man.

'Even were I to slaughter a thousand kingdoms,' he said, 'I would not have the power to do what you have just done.'

'A miracle from the heavens!' Ali Baba swooned.

Her face streaming with tears, Aladdin threw her arms around Scheherazade.

The others gasped again as Aladdin and Scheherazade hugged.

'Woman to woman!' the queen laughed.

Sindbad looked at Baibar, who glanced at Ali Baba.

All three of them looked at Aladdin questioningly.

'All right! I'm a woman!' she snapped.

Ali Baba and the Black Jinn gasped for a third time.

'When did you cease being a man?' asked Sindbad.

'I never was a man!' Aladdin exclaimed.

Baibar clapped his hands.

'We all have our secrets!' he said firmly.

Scheherazade tapped a fingertip to the coco de mer.

'We have to get to the palace!' she called.

Hurrying through the city's gate, the queen led the way.

A turn to the left, then a right, and another left, and they reached the great portal, at which the royal guard were standing to attention.

'We'll never get past them!' Ali Baba said.

'Why don't we go in the back door?' Sindbad asked.

'Because there isn't one,' the queen replied. 'Shahriyar had it blocked up, so that no one could break in.'

'If I could flatten an anthill,' Baibar announced, 'I could get my strength back, and turn those guards to dust.'

The story's seed still in her hands, Scheherazade held up a forefinger.

'I have an idea,' she said.

Thirty-six

A FEW MINUTES passed, and five female pilgrims dressed in sackcloth robes arrived at the palace gate.

As soon as he set eyes upon them, the chief of the guard ordered the visitors to stand aside.

'But we have brought a gift for King Shahriyar,' the first of the women said.

'A sacred gift,' added the second.

'Which will give him a long life and a thousand sons,' the third spoke.

Knowing the king to be superstitious, the official sent word for the king's vizier to attend the pilgrims, so that he could decide.

As soon as he saw the visitors, the vizier rolled his eyes.

'You will have to leave,' he said. 'The king's not in the mood to receive anyone.'

'But we are humble pilgrims from far away!' Baibar cooed, having adopted the guise of a pretty young woman.

'No excuses, and that's that!'

The vizier was about to turn on his heel when he caught the eye of a woman standing behind the others.

Dressed in a pilgrim's robe, Scheherazade pushed forward.

'Father,' she whispered, 'we must get into the harem. For if we don't, every young woman in the kingdom is at risk of losing her life, including me.'

'*Scheherazade!*' the vizier hissed. 'What games are you playing?!'

'Trust me, father.'

The chief adviser grimaced.

'What do you know that I do not?' he asked.

'I know the future,' his daughter replied.

Reluctantly, the vizier took charge of the pilgrims, leading them into the palace. But as soon as they were inside, he was called away to meet the king.

No stranger to the royal citadel, Scheherazade led the way to the harem.

As they turned the corner, they spied three burly guards blocking the way.

Undeterred, Aladdin strode up to the guards and fluttered her eyelashes, with Baibar in the form of a lovely girl following close behind. Next came Ali Baba, and Sindbad the Sailor, both of them dressed as women.

While the others diverted the guards' attention, Scheherazade slipped into the harem, tugging off her sackcloth robe once inside.

All around were beautiful young maidens: some of them bathing in the pool of crystal-clear water, others picking grapes from the enormous platters of fruit, or chasing one another around, laughing.

As she made her way through the harem, one of the young women, Leila, recognized Scheherazade. The two had been childhood friends. Running up, she gave the visitor a hug.

'I didn't know you were one of the king's attendants!' she exclaimed.

Fretfully, Scheherazade hurried around the pool of water, Leila giving chase.

'I can't stop,' she said, the coco de mer clutched to her chest.

'Let's gossip for a moment!' Leila pleaded. 'I've so much to tell you!'

'Later! First I must give a message to the queen.'

Scheherazade reached the royal apartment, with Leila still at her heels, begging her to stop for a chat.

A pair of eunuchs with arms crossed barred the way.

'I have a surprise gift for the queen!' Scheherazade cried. 'Here it is, see… a fine coco de mer from the distant shores of Africa.'

'The queen sees no one!' the guards said as one.

Scheherazade implored them:

'Please allow me in! I beg you!'

The guards held firm, refusing.

Calming herself, Scheherazade closed her eyes for a fleeting moment, and wished harder than she had ever wished for anything.

The ring on her finger began to warm… the sacred relic of the miniature Grilliax people, whose kingdom was a tree in a hole on an island far away.

It grew warmer and warmer as though it had been activated.

The pair of towering guards vanished – just like that.

A moment later, Scheherazade was inside the royal apartment, a chamber she'd known only in times of terrible fear. Nearby, the king's first and only queen was reclining on the bed, fragrant rose petals sprinkled all around.

'Hello,' she said sleepily. 'Have you come with more fruit?'

'No, I haven't,' Scheherazade answered. 'I've come to save your life, and that of more than a thousand women, including me.'

The queen sat up, a look of bewilderment on her face.

'Sit here beside me,' she said, 'and explain it all.'

So, Scheherazade sat on the corner of the bed, and told the queen about her husband's rage; how he'd given the order for her to be executed, and how – night after night – he had married a new bride at dusk, and had her beheaded at dawn.

At that moment there was a tapping sound on the window.

The queen flinched.

'That's him,' she said sobbing, her eyes heavy with tears. 'The young man who's been wooing me. He would have climbed up onto the balcony.'

'Please! Order him to leave!'

'But he's infatuated with me. He won't leave!'

Scheherazade smiled wryly.

'Don't worry, I am sure he'll see sense,' she said.

Just then, there was the roar of a monster below the balcony – as loud as ten thousand tigers.

'Whatever could that be?!' the queen spluttered.

'I have a feeling it's a friend of mine named Baibar... doing what I asked him to do.'

Scheherazade made the queen promise never to even look at another man, and certainly not to allow herself ever to be wooed. Striding over to the magnificent hourglass, she ran a hand over it.

'Like many men, he suffers from certain insecurities,' she said. 'He's prone to jealousy and cruelty on an unimaginable scale. Just as he's capable of great love, he's capable of terrible revenge as well.'

Scheherazade made her way over to the long window and strode out onto the balcony.

Then, peering down into the darkness, she leapt off.

Thirty-seven

HAVING TRANSFORMED BACK to himself again, Baibar reached out with all four arms, and caught Scheherazade, who was still clutching the story's seed.

A dazzling flash of light.

The pair found themselves in a caravanserai in the middle of the desert, the nocturnal firmament glinting above.

Sitting before them on a carpet were three familiar faces – Ali Baba, Aladdin, and Sindbad the Sailor.

As soon as they appeared, a cheer went up.

'I think we did it,' Scheherazade whispered.

'*You* did it,' the Black Jinn answered.

'We just came along for the ride,' Aladdin laughed.

Hot mint tea was served, as the travellers recalled the adventures and the narrow escapes.

'Thank God for the story seed,' Ali Baba said all of a sudden.

Scheherazade paused, shook it from side to side, and said:

'I wonder...'

'Wonder *what?*' Aladdin asked.

Without answering, she slid her thumb into the base, opening it up. Then, while the others watched in the moonlight, she pulled back a little hatch at the bottom of the coco de mer and fished out a scroll.

'What's that?' Sindbad asked.

'No chance of reading it until morning,' she said.

Baibar coughed into his fist, and the full moon shot out a spotlight, which illuminated Scheherazade's hands.

Regarding him with disapproval, she gave thanks as she unfurled the scroll.

'My God.'

'What is it?' Sindbad queried.

'It's a story,' she said. 'It's *our* story... the one which began with four strangers setting off from a distant caravanserai to save the life of a queen.'

The Black Jinn turned the moon's light down, and they all sat in silence for a long while.

'What will each of you do now?' Scheherazade asked.

Ali Baba spoke first:

'I shall get a little shop in the city and live quietly,' he said.

'I think I'll become a storyteller,' Aladdin replied. 'Our adventures have given me plenty of material.'

Sindbad peered through the darkness at the horizon.

'And I shall go to sea,' he said.

'What about you, Baibar?'

'Well,' the jinn uttered modestly, rubbing his single eye, 'I do believe I shall live as quietly as I can... until I'm needed by one of you.'

Scheherazade let out a shrill laugh.

'We humans have a way of getting ourselves into trouble,' she said.

'Can I ask what you will do?' the jinn rejoined.

The former queen sighed.

'I think I'll wait and see what Providence sends my way.'

At that moment, the ring on her finger warmed, and

something appeared in the distance, floating through the air towards the caravanserai.

'What's that?' said Aladdin fearfully.

Leaping up, Baibar got ready to protect his friends.

'Oh my,' Scheherazade gasped.

'It's King Arsalan!' cried Aladdin.

As they watched, the carpet came to a halt a short distance away.

The monarch spoke a greeting.

'I do hope you don't mind me intruding,' he said courteously, 'but I just happened to be passing.'

'Really?' Sindbad asked.

'Yes.'

'You happened to be flying over the very same caravanserai where we happened to be enjoying a glass of tea?' asked the sailor in disbelief.

King Arsalan let out a chuckle.

'As I told you,' he said, 'the story's seed lay in the treasure vaults beneath my family's palace for a thousand years. As a child, I found it there, worked out how to open it, and I read the tale which I see you have yourself discovered.'

'It's the story of our adventures,' Scheherazade said.

'And as you have no doubt seen, there's a happy ending.'

'I haven't yet got to the end.'

'Oh,' said King Arsalan.

Scheherazade unfurled the scroll and, glancing at Baibar, she cleared her throat. The Black Jinn clicked the fingers on one of his paws and the full moon sent out a dazzling spotlight again.

'"And so it was that Sindbad the Sailor embarked on a new adventure, with the deep ocean beneath the keel of his ship. Ali Baba went into business with an emporium of fine goods, and knew abundance and joy. Aladdin had more adventures, became a storyteller and, at last, settled down as the beautiful young woman she was. And Baibar remained the truest friend to them all."'

'Is that it?' Sindbad asked.

'Almost…'

'Go on…'

Her voice trembling as it spoke the words, Scheherazade read:

'"Once their journey was finished, the travellers took refreshment at a distant caravanserai in the light of a full moon. Having discussed their plans for the future, they spied something flying towards them through the darkness… a magnificent carpet, upon which was sitting a king. His name was Arsalan. And, having given greeting, he bowed deeply, and asked the question he had travelled across a hundred horizons to ask."'

King Arsalan bowed in reverence.

'Dearest Scheherazade,' he said, the moonlight glinting in his eyes, 'please be my queen and make me the happiest man in the world.'

Finis

A REQUEST

If you enjoyed this book, please review it on your favourite online retailer or review website.

Reviews are an author's best friend.

To stay in touch with Tahir Shah, and to hear about his upcoming releases before anyone else, please sign up for his mailing list:

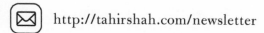 http://tahirshah.com/newsletter

And to follow him on social media, please go to any of the following links:

http://www.twitter.com/humanstew

@tahirshah999

http://www.facebook.com/TahirShahAuthor

http://www.youtube.com/user/tahirshah999

http://www.pinterest.com/tahirshah

https://www.goodreads.com/tahirshahauthor

http://www.tahirshah.com

Lightning Source UK Ltd.
Milton Keynes UK
UKHW011916170621
385696UK00002B/88